Mr. Mrs. R.B. Johnston
131 Princeton Rd.
Nashua, New Hampshire

Cecily Crowe

The Tower of

Kilraven

Holt, Rinehart and Winston · New York Chicago San Francisco

For Camilla

The Tower of Kilraven

1

How unused, Carlotta pondered irresponsibly, Americans had become to crooked teeth in the young. It was the snaggled array before her rather than the green, white, and orange flag flapping sociably over the air terminal that marked her arrival in a foreign land. These teeth and one other thing (for all airports seemed anonymous), a subtle permeating odor, musky and melancholy, somehow prehistoric, which she had noticed when she emerged from the plane : peat smoke, perhaps?

The young man with the terrible teeth was explaining the complicated reverse gear of the little car she was about to rent. "I'll get used to it," she promised, pulling herself together, for he had come to a halt under her dull stare. "I'm a bit groggy now, you see."

Readily he commiserated. "Of course, after a night flight and with the difference in time as well." He was partial to American ladies, who invariably returned his company's cars unscathed, and this Mrs. Fleet had pleasing eyes as well. Briefly he summed things up—keys, maps, rental papers. "So I'll leave you now and good luck to you!"

And a few minutes later she was puttering cautiously along the left side of the concrete road bordering the airport, and it wasn't until she reached the end of the runway, nearly a mile from the terminal, that she stopped the car and shut off the motor and gave herself up to realizing the moment.

A silence, scarcely broken by the murmurings of invisible, unfamiliar birds, awaited her—the silence of the close, clouded sky, a sky as omniscient, as personal, as a presence. It was not a foreign country after all. For she seemed to recognize in her bones this silence, this close sky with its musky fragrance and its muted voices, and knew it was the pervading influence of this land. Freshly charged with Yeats, Synge, and the legends, a pilgrim on a pilgrimage and with all the makings of a romantic, she thought she could hear the voices—of bards and warriors and keening women.

"I'm here!" Carlotta Fleet announced exultantly, as many another pilgrim before her had saluted an ancestor. "I'm in Ireland!"

"What would you do now," Dr. Fred had asked her, "if you could do anything you wanted to?" It was a question which seldom failed to bring a light into the eyes of a listless patient.

If he had been twenty years younger and not already comfortably married he might well have asked, "And now will you marry *me?*" The estate of her recently deceased husband had been settled, his wardrobe disposed of, and acknowledgments of sympathy written, and Dr. Fred had seen her through her subsequent collapse which took the form of flu. This afternoon he perched, all folded limbs like a praying mantis, in her sunny south parlor, drinking coffee and casting about for a way of getting her to pick up the threads of life again or, better still, to start afresh.

"I'd dye my hair blonde and go to Ireland," she answered automatically, almost indifferently, as if it were a dream she had long ago resigned herself to not realizing. No special light brightened her eyes. They were endowed

10

in fact with a permanent luminousness peculiar to gray-green eyes, sleeplessness or flu notwithstanding, and although pale and underweight, she was a wistful, proposal-evoking figure in the large wing chair.

"Ireland!" he shouted, typically ignoring the half of her wish to do with aesthetics.

"And why not?" She suddenly sat bolt upright, her eyes widening; his homely therapy was working after all. "Why, I ask you, not?"

"But why Ireland?"

"Because my mother's name was Athlone, and I've always had a hankering to see the land of my ancestors." It was a pilgrimage Harry, her late husband, had declined to share, as he was of Dutch extraction and required more concrete objectives. "And now I could go, couldn't I?"

"I wish I'd known," he complained, thrusting aside his cup, "about this Athlone strain before." His gray hair was not so much crew cut as streamlined for action, and he wore bow ties. "It accounts for a lot of your vagaries. Yes, you could go now, and why don't you?"

She subsided, bit her lip. New England conditioning and Harry's caution reclaimed her. "Well, there's so much to do . . ."

"*What's* to do?"

"There's the garden to tend to, and spring cleaning, and I hate to miss the lilacs—"

"You're thirty-seven and you're beginning to talk like an old maid. Harry was sick a long time, I needn't remind you, and you've been leading too circumscribed a life. You haven't even been to Boston lately." His reference to Harry's illness had brought a warning blur to her eyes but he blundered on. "And, yes, damn it, I might add too circumspect. Go ahead and—*what*, dye your hair blonde, did you say?" He threw up his gangling arms and now she was beginning to smile. He really hated to part with her, en-

11

courage her to go off into the blue like this, drive past her fine old house at the end of the green and know she was not in it, but he wouldn't have her dying on the vine. "Go ahead, go ahead, take the plunge, have a ball. Take your sketch pad and paints. Take your field glasses. Keep an open mind. Who knows, you might meet with adventure!" He got his feet under him and unfolded to his full height. "Just what the doctor would have ordered, had he known of Miss Athlone." He paused at the door and frowned. "But you will come back, won't you?"

So Carlotta closed her house, turned her back on her flower beds and budding lilacs, and went to New York, where she innocently put herself into the hands of Lucille, Harry's sister, a nervous woman possessed of travel experience, fashion knowledge, and executive tendencies.

"No, you must not dye your hair blonde," Lucille decreed at once. "You have a natural copper tint which sets off your eyes, and you don't want to be stuck in a castle with darkening roots."

"Castle?" It had been Carlotta's ingenuous plan to roam, sketching where the scenery appealed to her and stopping at picturesque old inns.

"There are no picturesque old inns in Ireland," her sister-in-law informed her. "There are hotels, either small commercial ones or vast Victorian ones. You will go straight to Kilraven Castle, which you can make your headquarters for side trips. Lady Kilraven takes paying guests, but only by introduction. Sad," she commented, in an unemotional aside. "What with the family tragedy and all. I will write Lady Kilraven," she stated with a steady, rather unreliable stare, "that you are coming. And now we must get rid of these—*provincial* clothes, and buy you a wardrobe."

12

And thus it was that Carlotta found herself meditating at last at the end of the runway of Shannon Airport.

It was May and the gorse was golden and the hawthorn blossoms pink and white. She drove on between high hedges and glimpses of sheep grazing in rolling fields, as lushly green as ever promised, and the sky traveled also, lowering and breaking open to reveal white heights of cloud and closing again. She stopped once to ask directions. A black-haired policeman, dismounting from his bicycle, dropped his dark eyes in deference, and from him came a dark melodious voice. "In fact," he said, and it charmed her that a policeman, in need of a shave, should begin a sentence with this soft and stately phrase, "in fact, ye're on the right road." Gently he brushed his *r*'s. "Ye'll come to a steep hill and the gates of the demesne will be on your left."

They exchanged amenities and she drove on. *Demesne*, she crooned, enchanted. The steep hill turned out to be what an American would call a grade, and at the foot of it a convex semicircle of yellow columns and black iron gates invited rather than excluded. The drive within wound for a long time through a natural park of low-hanging beeches and wild rhododendron, and then it mounted a rise and there across a lake was a neat, indisputable, and wholly gratifying castle.

Again Carlotta stopped her car, and at the same moment the sun broke through the clouds and turned the fanciful pile to silver and the lake to blue, reflecting the battlements. Kilraven Castle, founded in the Middle Ages by a member of the Fenn family, had been remodeled in the 1830's by Paine, a professional castle-restorer from Cork, and indeed, with its gray crenelated turrets and jaunty little flag surmounting all, it had a charming early-Victorian innocence.

13

But in the next instant the clouds closed again, the view cooled, and now, as if in a steel engraving in a novel by Sir Walter Scott, the castle in a twinkling was almost forbidding. The tall Neo-Gothic windows were blank and slate-colored, but Carlotta had a feeling she was being observed from them, and she wondered if she should have stuck to her original plans. "I do hope," she suddenly worried, "that Lucille remembered to write," for like many female executives Lucille showed an unnerving callousness toward minor details. With a little sigh Carlotta started up her car.

The drive led her around the lake and finally to a lawn as taut and thin as a bowling green. Her knees shaking now with exhaustion, Carlotta got out under the looming towers and mounted the stone steps to a Gothic porch. She straightened, summoning her last ounce of dignity, and pressed a bell, half-expecting it to be answered by an ancient castellan in doublet or jerkin.

The door at length swung inward on an apple-cheeked little woman in Harris tweeds.

Carlotta swallowed. "Lady Kilraven?"

"No-o-o," warbled the woman, ranging with the one syllable over almost an entire octave, "I am Miss Mims, her ladyship's secretary!" Her accent was one hundred percent English, and she cocked her head, its outlines misty in brown frizz, and pursed her lips in an uncertain yet somehow wily smile.

"I am Carlotta Fleet. My sister-in-law, Mrs. Blade, wrote you——?" The query died. Mrs. Blade had obviously not written, and for an instant Carlotta's fate hung in the balance.

But with a series of swift darts Miss Mims's bright eyes, almost black, took in Carlotta's elegant traveling costume, her shoes, bag, and gloves. "Mrs. Blade," Miss Mims murmured. "Of course! I remember. She *would* have

14

breakfast in her room." It was her traveling costume, Carlotta sensed, and not her sister-in-law's imperious ways, that got her by. The door suddenly widened. "*Do come in!*"

The vaulted interior of the porch served as a repository for boots and walking sticks, and there was a British Isles odor of damp floor matting. Vast eighteenth-century paintings of battle scenes leaned out from the dark upper reaches.

"We were *just* going in to lunch," said Miss Mims, leading the way up a second flight of stone stairs, "but I shall tell Lady Kilraven you've come."

Lunch? marveled Carlotta, for it was not long past dawn, American time, and she was scarcely able to face breakfast. They passed through another great door, and then they were in a long golden hall with a cluster of golden people at one end of it, all standing quite still in a leisurely, apathetic pose as if for a court portrait. Slowly all eyes turned to focus disinterestedly upon Carlotta, Miss Mims vanished in search of Lady Kilraven, and for a moment there was a trance-like silence. A large golden dog detached himself from the company and slowly advanced down the hall to her, slowly wagging a long tail, and she occupied herself with patting his head and staring helplessly into his sane, sentimental, golden eyes.

There was a little stir at last. The company parted and a high-backed chair came forward on wheels, seemingly self-propelled, and in it huddled, almost collapsed, a white-haired, white-skinned woman. The white lids, covering large eyeballs, lifted, and sky-blue eyes protruded. "I am Lady Kilraven," she moaned, "How do you do, Mrs. Fleet."

It was a semi-invalid's voice, strained and scratchy, conserving energy, giving a false impression of world-weariness and intimacy. Gently Carlotta grasped an ar-

15

thritic hand peaked like the scaffolding of a church roof.

"There has been a mistake," commenced Carlotta, dropping her voice to the same level, as though in conspiracy. Strangely, she wasn't intimidated by this collapsed but potent being; perhaps this was due to her own sympathetic state of near-collapse, or perhaps it was that with Lady Kilraven she found herself on a level of fundamentals all too familiar to her in her last year with Harry. "My sister-in-law promised to—"

"I have explained, I have explained!" caroled Miss Mims, popping out from behind the chair.

"You have explained," stated Lady Kilraven, quelling her with a stone-blue glance, and Miss Mims retreated. The eyes then studied Carlotta, not her clothes but her face, and some profound speculation, visionary rather than practical, seemed to occupy the elderly lady. She said at last, "It is quite all right, Mrs. Fleet. I'm glad you have come and you're welcome." There; in that sentence, her voice became low and beautiful, rich as the emerald fields. Miss Mims seemed shrill by comparison. Lady Kilraven's white, sagging cheeks, drawn downward by affliction, indicated a smile; obviously she could charm when she chose. "You are just in time for lunch."

"Will you excuse me?" Carlotta begged off. "I don't feel quite up to lunch. You see—"

"I do see. Many of our guests arrive from the night flight in this condition. You will want to get right into bed." Tears of gratitude sprang to Carlotta's eyes. But Lady Kilraven was again deliberating. "Miss Mims," she said, "the green room in the north tower, I think."

Miss Mims quickly emerged again. "Oh, but my lady, don't you think the pink room in the east wing?"

"I think the green room in the tower, Miss Mims."

There was an instant's silence. The golden company hung motionless in the background like a tapestry. Miss

16

Mims, still wearing her bright, all-purpose smile, was looking at Carlotta with unexpected, unreasonable antipathy. Now what on earth had brought all this about? Have done with it, Carlotta begged them silently, and let me get to bed.

"Very well, my lady," Miss Mims conceded in a whisper, and retired once more behind the chair.

"Have a good nap," said Lady Kilraven, dismissing Carlotta, "and we will see you at dinner." Her lids shut completely over her heavy blue eyes, her chair revolved slowly, and Miss Mims wheeled her away.

A few minutes later Carlotta was sinking under a down puff into the rocking, ear-ringing sleep of travel exhaustion. A tiny electric heater made a red eye in the darkened room. There was a knock, barely audible, and a teen-age maid with flaming cheeks thrust her head into the room to whisper in a stage brogue, "Wodyelikeahotwatherbotthle, madam?" which Carlotta could not translate. Gratefully she shook her head and the door silently closed. Jackdaws, or rooks perhaps, made hoarse stuttering noises in the battlements outside. She would have to look them up in her *Field Guide to the Birds of Britain and Europe*.

"I am in Ireland," she told herself, sinking. "I am in a tower in a castle in Ireland. . . ."

There was another knock, and Carlotta discovered from her traveling clock that it was nearly seven o'clock. The door opened and a lilac bush appeared.

"I *do* hope you've rested!" sang a familiar voice, now without a trace of animosity, and once again, having borne the mass of lilacs to a writing table, Miss Mims emerged. "Oh, yes, you *do* look so much better! I thought I should warn you we dine at eight, in case you feel up to coming downstairs." Busily she arranged the blossoms, but all the while her darting shoe-button eyes were taking

17

note of Carlotta's possessions. "Conor O'Connell is driving over; do you know his work? If there is anything you would like to have pressed, Mary will be happy to serve you."

"Can you mean the American Conor O'Connell, the writer?"

Miss Mims chuckled. "He is more Irish than American now, since making his residence in Galway. In fact, he's *rather* more Irish than the Irish. I *do* hope he's on his good behavior this evening." And leaving Carlotta to ponder this, Miss Mims smiled *au revoir* with a little quaking toss of the head and went away.

A corridor connected the tower to the main upstairs hall. Just to the left of Carlotta's door a narrow stair wound out of sight to a higher chamber, and beyond this stair a triangular bathroom hugged the curved wall of the tower. Opposite the bathroom a door was closed on another guest room.

But when Carlotta emerged from her bath it was open a crack and an eye was peering out. "Hi!" said a loud unabashed voice, and the door opened wider. A tall rangy woman, in a silk dressing gown, stood brushing her long gray hair. "Feeling better?"

"Oh, yes, much better, thanks."

"Saw you when you arrived, green in the face. Like a little nip before dinner? They serve drinks in the library but the atmosphere is very square, as my daughter would say. I'll pop over to your room after a while. See you." The door closed.

Carlotta had finished dressing and was putting things in an evening purse when the woman knocked. She wore a chinchilla wrap over a short dress of green brocaded satin, her hair was expertly pinned up in a French twist, and she strode forward and thrust out a freckled, diamond-studded hand. "I'm Fran Malloy." She had comfortably

18

broad hips but her arms and legs were like pipestems. "We're from St. Paul. J.J., my husband, is off looking up relatives in Donegal with our daughter, Sheilah. They'll be back tomorrow. J.J. has a fondness for tracing distant cousins and connections, and I have a weakness for titles and castles. You look gorgeous."

"Why, thank you." Carlotta was wearing a frock of coffee-colored lace, another of Lucille's dictates, flattering to Carlotta's undyed hair and strikingly unprovincial about the neck and bosom.

"Scotch," said Fran, producing a bottle from under her chinchilla. "I've been here a week, but I haven't acquired a taste for Irish yet." She strode to the washstand and busied herself with glasses. "I'm not much of a drinker, really, but I like getting acquainted and down there in the library I have to concentrate on not talking too loud. Dr. Fabret considers me a roaring extrovert, no doubt, and that's all right with me."

"Dr. Fabret?"

"Headshrinker from Boston. You'll meet him when we go down. All brain, few words, scares Sheilah; I think he's a lamb. Here's to you!" She perched on the arm of a chair by the hearth. "Now let's hear something about yourself."

It was still daylight outside, for in Ireland in May the sun sets at nine. Long windows on either side of the dressing table commanded a view of the lake. The sky had cleared and the slanting sun glittered on the water.

Carlotta, aware of the prosaic nature of her own particulars, identified herself briefly. "Tell me more about the other guests, Mrs. Malloy."

"Fran! Fran!" she shouted. "Nobody ever calls me Mrs. Malloy except Mr. Malloy, when I get too bossy. You want a rundown on the establishment. Well, guests come and go, a batch left today after lunch, and May is a

19

little ahead of the season, so for the time being there's just you and I and Dr. Fabret. Oh, and Conor O'Connell is coming for dinner. He's something of a West Country celebrity and he *has* acquired a taste for Irish. You may therefore meet Moira Fenn, who has some sort of thing going with O'Connell. The Fenns live in a cottage of their own on the other side of the demesne." Fran swung a long foot beautifully shod in green brocade to match her dress. "Dermot Fenn is Lady K.'s nephew, and he manages the demesne for her—the outdoors of it, the farms and stables and so on. He may drop in to collect Moira, but otherwise he's fairly antisocial. Plus Miss Mims and Lady K., that's the story."

"Lord K.?"

"Deceased. You'll see his portrait in the dining room. They look alike. Lady K. was a Fenn, too, you know—they were cousins. You have to hand it to her, keeping a grip on everything, even from a wheel chair, and making everything run smoothly. She had some kind of stroke or heart attack not long ago, on top of her arthritis."

"She is impressive," Carlotta agreed. "I have an idea she can even decide whom she wants to like her."

Fran grinned. "And judging from the little scene in the hall today I'd guess Lady K. has decided she wants *you* to like her."

"I had the same feeling. And I do like her." She hesitated. "So far. She doesn't reveal herself all at once, does she? There was something about a family tragedy. Was it her husband?"

"I wouldn't say from his portrait he was the tragic type, all mustaches and medals, and anyway he died a natural death in the Thirties. No, it was her son. He was killed in one of those pointless automobile smash-ups. Her only child—and talented, too, I gather. And don't ask me how I picked all this up because no one mentions him

20

and no one asks questions, not even me." Somewhere below a gong reverberated and Fran stood up, five feet ten in heels. "And since I don't believe in ghosts I haven't seen him wandering around here at night either, as he is supposed to do from time to time."

Conor O'Connell, decided Carlotta, was on his good behavior but not enjoying it. The mood at dinner had been easy and somewhat facetious, one calculated no doubt by Lady Kilraven to bring strangers together, and no one was inclined to give the renowned, tormented man the floor. Only Carlotta, who alone had not met him before and thought his large grizzled head and pock-marked face had something of the helplessness and humiliated grandeur of the faces on Mount Rushmore, appeared to take him seriously. He could lead brilliantly a conversation initiated by himself, but one set off by others left him one jump behind, and he fell back on peevish silences and *non sequitur* pronouncements, and as the meal wore on he developed a fruity brogue.

Now, following dinner, everyone had paired off in the gold and white drawing room, Fran Malloy and Lady Kilraven bending over a map in a box-shaped bay window, and Miss Mims, knitting, delivering a monologue in an undertone to Dr. Fabret, who sat on the sofa beside her with his eyes closed and his head tilted back like a sunbather. Moira Fenn drifted off to the piano to play wistful Noel Coward tunes in an unskilled but stylish manner. Carlotta therefore was O'Connell's only audience, but since she had as yet no established prestige he aimed his remarks over her head to the room at large.

"Sure, and Yeats was the greatest poet since Shakespeare," he proclaimed, leaning against the mantel in a red *bainin* jacket, Peterson pipe in one hand and Jameson drink in the other. No one paused or turned, and only the late, walrus-mustached Lord Kilraven bent his hyper-thyroid gaze on him.

"I wonder," responded Carlotta cautiously, seated on the hearth bench and feeling called upon out of courtesy to challenge him, "if Yeats himself would agree with you." And Dr. Fabret opened one eye and rolled it in her direction.

With a start O'Connell transferred his focus to her. A triangular patch of maroon appeared over the bridge of his nose, and he drew himself up to launch an annihilating reply. But from where he stood, he discovered just then, he had a charming view of her décolletage, and just at that moment Moira Fenn, aware of some change in the wind, paused at the piano and turned her tawny head.

He bent lower. "Your regard for Yeats then is serious altogether," he said meltingly, "for in truth he had no need of extravagant claims. Shall we go and pay our respects to his resting place in County Sligo? 'Tis but a half day's drive. Y'must let me drive ye there someday soon."

"Well, perhaps," Carlotta hedged, mindful of a cross-current between O'Connell, suddenly winning, and Moira, some distance away, openly listening. "Someday when the weather is good."

"Ha!" said Moira, arching her aristocratic golden eye-brows. She rose, tossing back her thick hair, and swinging her thighs in leisurely arcs moved to reach a cigarette urn on the coffee table between the two fireside sofas. She wore a silvery crocheted dress and in it her body, strong, supple, and large-boned, was like ancient sculpture. "She's waiting on the weather, is she?" she continued, lisping her s's as she lighted a cigarette. "When the sun shines in Sligo, Mrs. Fleet, it's raining in Drumcliffe."

"The sky changes in Ireland," explained O'Connell tenderly, "from hour to hour, from moment to moment."

It was as if, thought Carlotta, everyone had taken to uttering blank verse.

"And the sky is all that changes, Mrs. Fleet," concluded Moira, an oddly bitter smile on her long, suntanned face. "All else is predictable, to be sure." She turned her back and strolled toward the bay. "What are you plotting, Aunt Augusta? Surely not a visit to a grave?" And Fran Malloy let out a whoop of protest.

" 'Cast a cold eye on Life, on Death,' " murmured Dr. Fabret unexpectedly, and O'Connell seized the opportunity to go and replenish his glass, an action Miss Mims's bright, dark eyes did not fail to observe. Hannan, the sleek-haired butler, came to call Miss Mims to the telephone, and Carlotta moved with relief to the sofa on the other side of the doctor.

He was in his thirties, perhaps, although his dark hair was already threaded with gray, and he wore glasses with heavy black rims. Carlotta had earlier felt a kind of mental static emanating from him, an electric fuzz of cerebral activity, but whatever his thoughts he kept them to himself and was not given to small talk.

"Do you believe in ghosts?" Carlotta ventured.

"No," he replied. "Do you?"

"No."

And they lapsed into silence. But after catering to the tortured ego of Conor O'Connell and once again finding herself caught up in unfathomable hostilities, Carlotta was content to be quiet.

"What amuses you?" asked Dr. Fabret presently, his face still tilted ceilingward.

"Here I am, literally dropped out of the sky, in an Irish castle. It's like finding myself in the first act of a play. A week ago I was scurrying about trying to leave my house in order—closing the dampers against the chimney swifts, hiding soap from mice, homely things like that. Now the curtain rises. A mixed company is gathered in the drawing room . . ."

"Downstage center," he took her up, "sits a lady from New England, a newcomer with the look of reliability. Already the characters are beginning to bounce their feelings off her. Perhaps she is going to be the catalyst."

"Heaven forbid. No, much more likely the doctor sitting next to her, observing everything with his eyes shut."

He straightened, smiling. "What brought you here?"

"A mystic feeling for the island."

"Is that another quotation?"

"Yes, it was spoken by an Irish policeman. I stopped him this morning to ask directions. When I told him I'd just arrived and tried to tell him why, that is how he explained it for me."

"Where else in the world would a policeman use the word *mystic?*"

"And also," confided Carlotta, regarding her clasped hands, "it was pointed out to me at home, in the kindest possible way of course, now that I am a widow, that if I stayed on fussing with gardens and curtains and things—"

"Chimney swifts and mice."

"—why I was in danger of becoming ingrown and dull. An old maid, in fact. It was suggested I go off in search of adventure. They were doctor's orders, practically."

"Time-honored," nodded Fabret.

"Do you think adventure can really change the natural tendency of a person's life?"

"Perhaps it can make a quiet life more satisfying."

"That is a very discreet and sensible reply. And you, Dr. Fabret? What brought you?"

"Ah . . ." He hesitated a fraction of a second, as if he was more used to asking the questions. "The World

Conference of Neuropsychiatrists in Dublin, now adjourned, for one thing, and perhaps a curiosity about mystic feelings, for another."

Carlotta had no reason to suspect this was not the truth, but she sensed it was not quite the whole truth. "You haven't come here to exorcise the ghost?"

He smiled faintly. "It wouldn't be so far out of my line, would it? You might almost call me an exorcist."

"Have you been listening to gossip, Mrs. Fleet?" It was Miss Mims, who sat knitting again on the sofa opposite them. "Has our little legend reached you so soon?" Her jolly round face shone, and she smiled, and the slight tremor of her hands, gripping the needles, was barely noticeable.

In the back of her mind then Carlotta made a split-second decision, that she was not going to be put out of humor by Miss Mims. "You can't believe I took it seriously," Carlotta answered mildly. "Besides, I thought most castles were proud of their ghosts."

"And you can't believe," a new voice, genuinely Irish, added behind them, "that Mrs. Fleet listens in on other people's conversations, as is the custom in Kilraven Castle."

Miss Mims flushed a strawberry red, and Carlotta turned.

A fair-haired man in rustic riding clothes, his legs gaitered and his elbows patched, stood hunched wryly over his folded arms, eying them with a smile. A line from Somerville and Ross, whose hilarious, Hibernian works Carlotta knew almost by heart, came to her: "He looked like a stable boy among gentlemen, and a gentleman among stable boys. . . ." For an instant no one made a move, and he introduced himself to Carlotta bluntly, suddenly stepping forward and thrusting a calloused hand over the back of the sofa. "Dermot Fenn," he said, and

25

Carlotta looked briefly into blue eyes, slightly hooded, very much like Lady Kilraven's. Then with a light, unhurried step, on the balls of his feet, almost feminine, or feline, in its co-ordination, he moved away to his aunt, whose crippled hand he bent to kiss in serious, schoolboyish homage.

Carlotta was aware of a sudden change in the atmosphere. Where it had been sultry, with everyone isolated by cross-purposes, it was now crisp, more alive with challenge, less heavy-hearted. Dermot Fenn had brought a tension with him like a breath of fresh air.

"Did the books balance, darling?" asked Moira, heedless of those present who were not members of the family. She looked handsome and dangerous, as if she had achieved this evening without him a potent identity which she must wave before him like a banner. "How stands Kilraven demesne? Will it hold together another year, another day? Can you spare it another drop of your life's blood?"

"Moria, behave," said Lady Kilraven quietly from the bay, as if this were an admonishment she had made before.

"Go on playing," said Dermot Fenn to his wife. "I haven't heard you play in an age. 'Twas that I came in to hear, not your impudence."

"In the wilds of Connemara," announced Fran Malloy, "day after tomorrow, J.J. and I are giving a picnic. You are all to come."

"I loathe picnics," said O'Connell, leaning against the piano.

"You'll come anyway," said Fran. "We'll fetch you. Show me on the map where you live."

Dermot Fenn had moved again to make peace with Miss Mims on the sofa. She giggled helplessly, and the ungainly golden dog with the long tail came padding shyly into the room, steering straight for Fenn. They communed, and Carlotta realized too late that her eyes, just as Fenn's lifted to meet hers, hadn't left him since he first spoke. He caught her stare with a look, lasting less than a second, of surprise, speculation, and amusement, and then with a slight deepening of the russet in his cheekbones his eyes dropped to the dog again and Carlotta's lowered too. Miss Mims was getting to her feet. Lady Kilraven was saying good night, and everyone rose and began moving with her wheel chair to the door.

"Don't forget," breathed O'Connell dragging on Carlotta's arm. "We have a date in County Sligo to put a flower on a grave."

For one dazed moment brought on by the return of fatigue, the fumes on O'Connell's breath, and trying to follow the shifting currents around her, she was tempted to answer him in rhyme, but Moira was studying them with a twist of the lips, and Dermot put an end to it by saying shortly, "Good night to you all," and drawing his wife away.

"You'll sleep well, Mrs. Fleet."

"Yes, Lady Kilraven, I shall. I'm grateful to you for taking me in without notice."

Again the blue eyes, bluer than her nephew's and more pronouncedly hooded, rested penetratingly on Carlotta's face. "Perhaps," she said in her low, strained voice, "your coming in this way was an omen, a good omen." The black, skeptical eyes of Miss Mims danced just behind and above her. Lady Kilraven signaled and Miss Mims urged the wheel chair forward and the remaining guests filed after.

"You'll have no trouble following doctor's orders," murmured Dr. Fabret, and a quick laugh broke from Carlotta.

In their corridor Fran said, "Sweet dreams, dear. You

won't mind being all alone in your tower? Bang on my door if you get nervous. Night-night."

An army of ghosts howling and clanking chains couldn't have disturbed Carlotta that night. It was all she could do to get through the ritual of toothpaste and skin cream. She drew back the curtains at last and opened the window. The out of doors was damp and dark and there was not a sound anywhere. Tomorrow she would explore. Her light made a patch on the grass below, and farther out there was another, narrower patch. Putting out her head and craning upward she was just in time to see a crack of light disappear behind a drawn curtain. She was not alone in the tower and had never really felt she was. Perhaps Mary, the maid with the flaming cheeks, lived upstairs. Carlotta went to bed, put out her light, and smiling unaccountably, was instantly asleep.

2

It was a pearly morning, giving the lie for the moment at least to the saying that the Irish sky is never empty. Not a cloud marred the heavens of May. A heart that seemed to have huddled for a long time in hibernation rose up in Carlotta's breast as if to sing. She was waiting for Fran on the front steps overlooking the drive and park. The shimmer of morning sunlight dazzled her, and the fragrance, the unique fragrance—of sod and foliage, of a softer air tainted always with the smoldering harvest of ancient bogs—welcomed her once more.

Buried, atavistic responses were coming from her with increasing intensity, the anonymous ancestral blood asserting itself, as if she were beginning to recognize a dwelling once lived in and loved in childhood. Was she fooling herself, she wondered? Was she superimposing sentiment on natural eagerness to respond? But feeling now seemed truer than rationality : it was instinct. She felt at home.

She had breakfasted in the high-ceilinged dining room with Fran, wistfully gazed upon by Fenns long past earthly hunger. The paneled walls were varnished orange and the fireplace was a Victorian-Gothic masterpiece of marble and fretwork, while the mahogany table, nearly twenty feet long and crowned with a centerpiece of blue lupine, was set with Georgian silver and Waterford crys-

29

tal. It was Carlotta's first opportunity to enjoy the ease of a self-service, sideboard breakfast. A proprietary eye rolled at them from time to time in the glass pane of the pantry door, but otherwise no servant and no one of the household was in evidence.

"Fabret eats early," said Fran, indicating the remains of a breakfast further down the table. She had been considerately silent until Carlotta poured her second cup of coffee. She wore a suit of subtle greenish tweed, and large gold bangles on her freckled wrists made a muted, 14-karat tintinnabulation. She pushed back her chair and lighted a cigarette. "Then he disappears for the morning. It is rumored that he is doing a report on the headshrinkers' conference for the American Headshrinkers' Journal. You slept well, didn't you?"

"Better than in months."

"Yes, you're really with us this morning." But as they were leaving the room Fran said, "He fascinates you, doesn't he?"

"Fabret?" gasped Carlotta.

Fran guffawed. "No, the man in the portrait. You just took a last look at him."

"Why, so I did." And Carlotta paused and turned again to the picture over the mantel.

A young man was seated conventionally against a landscape, but there was something at odds in both subject and painting. The young man, dark and scholarly, gazed with the now-familiar hooded blue eyes at the beholder with resentment, or some lack of equanimity, as if sitting for his portrait was an almost insupportable family duty. There was arrogance and, at the same time, extreme sensitivity in the arched black brows, weakness and stubbornness in the mouth, and the long, aesthetic hands that give the impression of cruelty. The painter, who revealed in the Irish landscape of the background that he was

30

capable of moving and highly personal work, must have been intimidated by the young man's scowl; the workmanship of the likeness was pure Royal Academy, slick, thin, and accurate, as if the painter had got it over with as soon as possible.

But what fascinated Carlotta, what emerged for her almost without her knowing it during breakfast as she continually glanced upward, was the proud, deeply reserved longing behind the scowl, a look of such profound despair that the skilled painter had caught it in spite of himself, lending its brooding to the background as well so that it colored the entire portrait. "It's the tragic only son, isn't it?" Carlotta murmured.

"It must be."

"What was his name?"

"Search me. I told you, they don't discuss him."

Something then told Carlotta they were being eavesdropped upon, and sure enough, emerging into the golden hall they found Miss Mims in her brown tweeds arranging the mail on a table close to the dining-room door with a bright, prepared smile. "Good morning, good morning!" she crowed. "And it *is* indeed a heavenly morning!" She was half-blocking their way. "And what are our plans for today?"

"*Dolce far niente*," said Fran, surprisingly, and adding to Carlotta, "Meet you on the front steps," she sidestepped Miss Mims, winked over her shoulder, and went up the staircase.

"Whatever did she mean by that?" giggled Miss Mims.

"It's sweet to do nothing."

"Indeed. Mrs. Malloy doesn't strike one as the idle sort, does she? I only wondered if you would be here for lunch or if you'd be wanting sandwiches put up."

"Sandwiches for me, please, Miss Mims." She made to move forward.

"Oh, but Mrs. Fleet." The little brown head tilted and the eyelids fluttered ingratiatingly. "I *do* wish to say, we have cozier, more attractive rooms available now, and Mary can move your things without inconveniencing you."

"I like the room I have, Miss Mims." And Carlotta realized her nails were digging into the palms of her hands.

"I see." Still smiling, Miss Mims drew her breath between her teeth. "But I am afraid, since your stay is rather indefinite——"

"Are you worrying Mrs. Fleet, Millicent?" It was Lady Kilraven, in a light aluminum chair which she was able to propel herself; she had come from a corridor leading from her ground-floor apartment. "She may stay where she is as long as she likes. I'll hear no more on the subject."

Miss Mims pursed her lips and her lids as well, and departed without another word.

"I couldn't get along without her, to be sure," said Lady Kilraven, obviously in a bright morning humor, "but she has gone the way of old household friends: she has become possessive and dictatorial. You must indulge her for my sake."

"I shall be happy to."

"And I, my dear, am happy to hear your stay is indefinite."

"Not really, Lady Kilraven. I planned a month's trip. But if you'd like me to be more specific . . ."

"I would like to make your stay so pleasant you'll not want to leave us at all." She studied Carlotta with a tiny smile; she seemed determined to interpret everything about Carlotta in the light of secret good fortune. Her face, wearing this smile, with its protruding, marblelike eyes and drooping lids, was somehow not reassuring. But instantly catching Carlotta's look of wariness, the eyes

32

melted and sparkled, the little smile spread, and Carlotta's face melted in response. "You're going out, of course?" asked Lady Kilraven. "Better go now before the clouds develop."

Waiting for Fran in the sunlight, Carlotta wondered what lay behind the charm of Lady Kilraven, the secret smile, the immense authority, the suffering—where, in other words, was the woman herself, the womanly woman, the sum of all her days, of girlhood and flirtation, passion, marriage, childbirth, sorrow, and aging? Carlotta was certain she was not inaccessible, that one needed only a clue or a key. The clue to Miss Mims, for example, was evident: her spinsterhood. But like the nine-tenths of an iceberg, the feminine motivation of Lady Kilraven, the source of her richness and the thread between her complexities, was yet to be uncovered.

"Got my clodhoppers on," said Fran, joining her. "Let's make the circle right around the castle. It's a good long hike." She took note of Carlotta's field glasses. "So you're a bird watcher. Somehow it figures." They set off along the drive. "I didn't mean to be nasty to little Miss Mims, but sometimes she bugs me."

Jackdaws croaked in the battlements overhead, and a dog barked somewhere, but otherwise the golden quiet of a sunny morning prevailed. Rounding the south tower they came upon a sheltered tennis court, and now the full depth of the castle's wings, of varying heights, materials, and periods, came into view. Small domestic dwellings clung feudally to the castle walls, and children came to stare at them with a smiling shyness from sunlit doorways.

"Come see the stables," said Fran, leading the way to an arch in a yellow wall. "Sheilah was bored with Kilraven till she discovered them. Isn't that the height of teen-age cynicism, being bored with a castle?"

They were about to pass into the cobbled courtyards when a woman's voice arrested them. "Damn it, you'll not sell Finn McCool."

Within the courtyard—a masterpiece of yellow brick and maroon trim—and mounted on a powerful gelding, Moira Fenn glared furiously down at her husband, who stood adamantly gripping the horse's reins. "He's more mine," continued Moira in a quivering voice, "than anything else in this bloody establishment. I'll go to your aunt about him."

"You'll not," answered Dermot Fenn, his hair shining red in the sunlight, "while she gives me charge. Finn McCool is ten years old, and five hundred pounds are five hundred pounds."

"Oh, God, is there no end to the penny-pinching! What do you expect me to ride at the Dublin show? Be damned to you!" And with a violence obscene to witness, she brought down her crop across his wrist, at the same time flinging her heels into the horse's flanks. Dermot let go with an international oath and the horse wheeled. Fran and Carlotta had already shrunk back in retreat, and now Moira clattered past, a white-faced blur in jodhpurs, her head bent to go under the arch, her lion-colored hair streaming.

"We will view the stables," muttered Fran, "some other time," and they tiptoed away.

"All is not blissful in this lovely demesne, is it?" murmured Carlotta, shaken by the nakedness of the scuffle.

"Is it anywhere?" asked Fran.

They rested on a stone seat in the walled Tudor garden. A stringent odor of box dominated the air. Wall flowers and lupine bloomed in rainbow colors, and moss made patterns on rose-colored brick. A laburnum tree in blossom stood lemon-yellow over the rose beds, and there were one or two of the incongruous palm trees of southwestern Ireland.

"Listen!" whispered Carlotta, gripping her field glasses.

"My God, what now?" whispered Fran.

A shivering, silvery cascade of notes sounded nearby, like an utterance, a distillation, of all the loveliness of May. "An English robin," Carlotta told her, sighting through her glasses. "The true robin."

Fran gave a sigh. "My hair is standing on end."

They came around the castle full circle. Clouds, thick as whipped cream, were at last beginning to mass in the sky. "J.J. and Sheilah will be getting back from Donegal," said Fran. "I'd better stick close to the house. Castle, I mean."

Carlotta fetched her water coloring gear and drove off. She had a sudden need to be alone, to lose herself among the hedged byways outside the demesne, and for an hour or more she toured the neighboring countryside, nervously avoiding cyclists and waving to red-headed children.

What unaccustomed longings, what intimations of emotions, long dormant, were awakening within her! She pulled up beside a blazing cover of gorse and a view of an ivy-covered ruin on a hill, one of the somber, pre-Cromwellian ruins that dot the landscape of Ireland, and ate her sandwiches. She thought of Harry, who had been so dear, stanch, and sensible. Had she ever given him this wayward woman of runaway feelings? Had she cheated him of her real self, or had she after all cheated herself of her real self? Tears filled her eyes momentarily, for she had loved Harry and it was her fervent hope that whatever self she had given him, she had made him happy. Whatever sentiments this country evoked in her, she hoped they would not in some way be a betrayal of him.

She was not without a sense of caution. Kilraven Castle

35

already presented vague pitfalls, such as Lady Kilraven's oddly conspiratorial manner, and Miss Mims's suspicion, to say nothing of her own incipient usefulness as a pawn in the conflicts between fringe members of the family, as evidenced the evening before. Her very sensitivity to the vibrations of emotion in others could be a danger. "Perhaps you are going to be a catalyst," the sphinx-like Dr. Fabret had suggested, a remark that today sounded uncomfortably like a warning.

She re-entered the black and yellow gates, came upon the vista of the castle across the lake, drew her car off the road and settled herself cross-legged on her raincoat. She hadn't tried her water colors in many months and she was rusty; she discarded a number of sketches before she got her hand in and her eye clarified. The sky was a water-colorist's dream with its opaque cloud masses, shadowed in slate blue, and she discovered that the green of grass and foliage, unlike the blue-green of New England, had an underlying darkness which demanded a preliminary brown wash. From time to time as she worked she unknowingly gave a sigh of contentment.

There was a brief flurry of traffic on the drive. A Bentley sedan traveled toward the castle at a confident speed, a plump, shiny-cheeked man in a tweed cap at the wheel and a pale blur of a girl beside him: J.J. Malloy, no doubt, and Sheilah, returning from their genealogical expedition to Donegal. A little while later, Miss Mims puttered away from the castle in a vintage two-seater and waved with a lack of surprise which indicated she already knew of Carlotta's whereabouts. Next, a dusty sports car rent the air with its intestinal roar and Moira Fenn swept by, looking neither to right nor left, also heading for the gates.

Then followed a long period of silence. Birds communicated with muted sibilance in the overhanging beeches, and demure brown rabbits emerged from their burrows to browse. Carlotta had reached that ticklish point in painting when a strong will to leave well enough alone is needed, before too many finishing touches produce disaster, and she was hesitating over her sketch when once again the self-conscious feeling of being observed from the castle stole over her.

She straightened, frowning. From where she sat she could see her own window in the north tower, half open as she had left it; but the window above it was opened wide, and its frame enclosed a vague form. On an impulse, with a hollow feeling in her throat, she took up her field glasses and trained them on the upper window.

There, a figure stood with field glasses trained upon her. Instantly their astonished mutual gaze broke off and the figure vanished.

A flush of perspiration broke out on Carlotta's forehead and neck and she put away her glasses. She was curiously short of breath and her heart thudded. She scowled. "All right, then," she said aloud, "go ahead and stare." And she made a face at the window, and took up her work again.

It was then that the golden dog came bounding up the rise toward her, perfunctorily scattering rabbits, and in its wake, walking thoughtfully with his hands in his pockets, came Dr. Fabret.

He didn't discover Carlotta until he was nearly abreast of her and then he said, "Oh, hello," absent-mindedly, and without another word, still absorbed in cerebral pursuits, turned onto the turf and dropped down in the shade close by. She, too, was preoccupied, lost once more in the artist's complicated double vision of subject and image, an exercise which creates its own timelessness, and they were silent.

At last she rested, easing the cramp between her

shoulders, and when he spoke she started and turned to him with a brush clamped between her teeth.

He said, "I always thought water colors were wishy-washy."

He leaned forward and took up the block with its finished painting and studied it through his heavy glasses. He wore gray flannels and a brown jacket and he might have stepped out of a faculty house on an American campus.

"Especially," she said, removing the brush from her teeth, "water colors painted by ladies."

"Yes," he agreed equably. He said after a moment, "This isn't wishy-washy at all." He handed it back, smiled at her, and leaned full length on one elbow.

She gave a gasp of laughter. "No one has ever appraised my work in quite those words."

"I know very little about painting," he answered, unabashed. "It's the painters who interest me."

"Of course." Something a little lofty, or smug, in his tone, threatening a flight into esoterics, made her decide contrarily to get down to basic truths. "But you can't really call me a painter. I'm just a dabbler, and I'm thankful to be one."

"All right. But this—dabble isn't just a pretty picture. It's very strong and sunny and mysterious."

"Is that so?" she said, curiously taking up the sketch again.

"Yes."

"You wonder what was going on in my subconscious mind?"

"Exactly." He was not to be mocked.

She looked up at the view, nibbling the end of her brush. "This is the way Kilraven looked to me when I first saw it—a fantasy, a Victorian fantasy, gay, with all that dark foliage around it; you could say this is the real Kilraven. But it isn't. It can also look very sad, as I found out when the sun disappeared, even sinister, spellbound, with a ghost in the tower."

He was silent a moment. "It would almost seem you take that ghost seriously."

His eyes, dark brown in his olive skin, regarded her with a smiling steadiness, as if he were enjoying a certain one-upmanship. Even Dr. Fred, Carlotta recalled, could be insufferable when he thought he knew more about her than she did herself.

"I do," she said. "Because I saw it a few minutes ago."

"*Did* you now," he answered quietly.

"We looked at each other through our field glasses."

He made a little snort. "Since when have ghosts come equipped with field glasses?"

Impatiently she put the sketch away in her portfolio and began to gather up her materials. "Oh, all right. It was one of the castle spies." She shivered suddenly and looked up. "There! The sun has gone under the clouds. Look! Do you see what I mean? Doesn't the castle look entirely different? Doesn't it look as if"—she stretched out her hands to it,—"as if it needed—"

"Yes?" he prompted softly, just behind her.

"Someone to break the spell!" She caught her breath and turned to him once more. "There is someone, a man, living in that tower."

"Is that supernatural?"

"No, but I have the feeling I'm not supposed to know about him."

"You think maybe they've got mad old Uncle Patrick up there in chains?"

She had to laugh. "I know. I'm being silly."

"I didn't say that."

He helped her to her feet, shook out her raincoat, and assisted her to her car. Her hands were full, and he took hold of her wrist to detain her. He asked, suddenly rather shy, "You're not troubled about this, are you?"

"No." She smiled. "Ever since I landed, my Irish blood has been playing havoc with my imagination."

"Your adventure mustn't be a troubled one. Why not leave family secrets, whatever they are, to the Kilravens?"

He released her, and she drove away, wondering. Did that, too, sound like a warning?

"For shame, staying indoors on such an evening!" The French doors of the drawing room were opened wide to the park, where the last of the evening sun gilded the tree-tops. Dermot Fenn stood looking in at the company, one booted foot on the sill, hands in pockets; he had appeared as if out of the forest, grinning, like a rustic half-man, half-sprite in a Shakespearean pastorale.

"He's got something there," said J.J., who had had enough of after-dinner sitting about anyway, and he sprang to his feet. "Come on, ladies, fetch your wraps and we'll step out."

"We might as well," said Fran, unhinging her long limbs. "J.J.'s a regular sheep dog when he wants ladies to move. He'll nip at your ankles."

Shorter than Fran, with a paunch and tiny feet, he was nevertheless commanding, for he had a cool eye and a narrow firm jaw under his plump cheeks, and more often than not he smoked a self-confident cigar. His wealth, Carlotta realized, was subtly revered in the Kilraven household.

Sheilah, however, showed only the most rudimentary signs of character, even at seventeen. Dainty of build and dimpled like her father, she might have been a vision of pearly skin, perfect American teeth, violet eyes, and fair hair, except that she seemed to be made of wax. Nothing seemed to register on her or in her. Mutely she suffered the conversation of her elders without the slightest involvement. She was little more than a pleasing displacement of air.

But as the others rose she found her voice long enough to mew, "Oh, Daddy, I've *rilly* had it. I've rilly got to hit the sack." She uttered slang as if it had been something learned respectably at boarding school along with a drawl and printed handwriting, and only Moira failed to wince. In fact the perpetual contempt in Moira's topaz eyes vanished only for Sheilah, and she appeared to hold the sated child in some curious respect.

"You've been a good sport, Kitten," said J.J., bestowing a kiss on Sheilah's virginal brow. "The Malloys of Donegal will never forget you."

Sheilah smiled wanly and, thought Carlotta, almost touchingly. Could it be that the child actually did suffer in the overpowering atmosphere of elderhood? "It was neat, Daddy." Fran had evidently been strict about her manners and Sheilah said good night prettily to everyone in turn. "I'll show you my Donegal tweeds tomorrow, Lady Kilraven, they're rilly d'vine." And turning to the company as a whole, she mistily swallowed a yawn and gave them her idiosyncratic farewell, half-affected and half-childlike, "Love-love!" And she went off to bed.

Dermot Fenn, with his sylvan smile, still waited, his boot on the sill. Fran had described him as largely antisocial, and he did appear to lend his presence now as the result of some whim, or as if he had been bewitched by the evening hour. They came out onto the terrace, and letting Moira lead the way with J.J. and Dr. Fabret, he fell in between Fran and Carlotta.

"If only this weather holds for our picnic," sighed Fran.

"The BBC," said Dermot, "predicts 'Showery with bright periods,' with its usual caution." And they laughed.

They crossed the green and took the wide path into the park. "You're coming with us tomorrow, Dermot?"

"Ah, Fran, how can I? Who would lay the whip to my lazy farmers?"

"Don't you ever take a day off?"

"For the races, to be sure, and a hunt now and then. Someone has to keep the place from falling to rack and ruin." It was a self-pitying refrain Carlotta was getting used to now from the Fenns, but at that moment a satirical eye met hers, as if challenging her. And he asked, "How did your picture turn out?"

"Not bad." Surely Dermot Fenn's duties did not include spying out of the north tower. "I should ask, shouldn't I, how you knew I was painting?"

He smiled. "Ah, there are eyes everywhere in Kilraven demesne. You'll get used to it in time." And a turn in the path brought his shoulder against Carlotta's; he was not very much taller than she. Almost, but not quite immediately, he moved away again.

It was then that Carlotta became fully aware of his disturbing effect on her. His slight muscular build, his unique grace, his complexity—the hints of cruelty and tenderness, boldness and shyness, all combined so harmoniously as to form a kind of animal simplicity—had a perilous appeal. Or was this, too, part of the enchantment of the evening?

Their voices had dropped with the increasing density and darkness of the woods, and to Carlotta they were like figures moving with the seeming normality of a dream. In the dusk ahead Moira led them between the mossy trunks and spreading branches, her long, slow stride setting her filmy chiffon skirt to fluttering, while a cacophony of evening bird song hovered over them in the still-gilded foliage like a canopy. Removed from time, removed from their separate, skeptical worlds, they were united in the ancient Irish forest.

"One can almost see faces among the ferns," breathed Carlotta.

"And why not?" said Dermot softly.

They came to a temple. A circle of slender, lichen-mottled columns, supporting a dome, crowned a little knoll. Temples were the usual thing in castle parks, Carlotta told herself, but there was a leafy, pagan silence in this clearing that made everyone halt expectantly. The last of the light filled the opening in the trees.

Letting fall her woolen stole, Moira ran lithely up the rise, her gown floating in the twilight. An instant later the temple held the statue it called for. Green as the shadows, one arm curved over her bowed head, her dress dropped to her waist, Moira stood transfixed.

Dermot's fists rose warningly to his hips. But the spectacle was too lovely, too serene, too much the green of the greening darkness, and no one spoke.

In another instant, Moira stepped down again, laughing, her dress in place. Fran looked shocked. "All right, Mother," scolded J.J., somewhat shocked himself, "the show's over."

"Usually she's a little drunk when she does this," said Dermot coolly, "and she takes all her clothes off."

Fabret sent Carlotta a quizzical glance over his glowing pipe. Moira rejoined them, breathing quickly, her eyes glittering at her husband.

"We'd better get back while we can see our way," advised J.J. sharply, and set off with Fran. Moira, bemused, took Fabret's arm. They walked again in silence, and now even the birds were still; an herbal fragrance issued from the dark shapes around them.

"You weren't offended?" asked Dermot, half-derisively.

"It was part of the dream," Carlotta answered.

They could see the lights of the castle through the trees. On the edge of the park a branch brushed Carlotta's head and Dermot's arm reached around her to lift the branch. The others moved on, crossing the lawn, but Dermot barred Carlotta's way and drew her forward to face him. "There is dew in your hair," he murmured, and the breath held still in her throat. He was smiling, his hands on her shoulders.

The sound of whimpering reached them then, as it had already reached the others, frozen in their tracks. Dermot wheeled. A pale figure came running from the castle across the lawn. The cries, broken by the jar of running, occupied the silent night like some lonely, demented jazz accompaniment. Sheilah in her nightgown and robe, emerging from the semidarkness, ran straight into her mother's arms.

"I saw it," she sobbed, in the hiccoughing way of children. "I saw it, I saw it, I saw it."

"Saw what, Kitten?" demanded J.J., very distinctly.

"The ghost. In Mrs. Fleet's room. I saw it."

The castle was quiet at last. Sheilah had been put to bed with a sedative, administered by Dr. Fabret. Miss Mims had hovered about with smelling salts, her teeth chattering, but it was Dermot who had taken charge and brought about order. It was generally agreed by all but Sheilah that what she had seen when she emerged from the triangular bathroom was the white glass curtains in Carlotta's room, stirring in the night air.

There was a knock on Carlotta's door. It was Dr. Fabret. "Do you want a pill, too?"

"No, thanks," she told him grimly.

He said, not quite looking at her, "Lock your door, will you?"

"And you said I was the one who was taking the ghost too seriously!"

He started to speak, thought better of it, started to leave; then he caught his breath and gave a little sigh. "I," he said, "am taking you seriously. Lock it, will you?"

"All right." They were standing on either side of the door, speaking in low tones, and perhaps because, when he did look at her, he found her eyes baffled, unafraid, and beautiful, he leaned forward and kissed her cheek reassuringly.

And then, somewhat surprised at himself, he said good night and quickly shut the door.

Nothing was missing from her portfolio, but it had been opened, the sketches disarranged. She took up the finished painting of the castle.

A night light burned dimly at the end of the hall. Carlotta waited outside her door for a long moment. A rich snore came from Fran's room.

She mounted the tower stairs. They were carpeted, steep and narrow, and they ended in almost total darkness at a door halfway around the tower again. No crevice of light showed, but Carlotta was able to slide the painting under the door until it vanished. Then she turned, trembling violently and out of breath, and hurried down the stairs to her room again. She locked her door and went to bed.

3

Sheilah sat with her chin in her hand, pale and still yawning from her sedative. She deserved a little fun, thought Carlotta, and wondered what, if anything, could bring the apathetic child to life. Hannan, the butler, was stowing hampers and rugs in the Bentley under J.J.'s nimble direction while the others waited on the castle steps. Moira, drawing up in her battered sports car, joined them, and Dr. Fabret had been persuaded to go along. From the top step, all smiles and sallies, Miss Mims waited to see them off.

Then, in the midst of seating arrangements, Dermot Fenn appeared on a tall, self-centered-looking horse. The dreamlike events and tendencies of the night before flitted at once through Carlotta's mind, with a skip of the pulse, but although Dermot drew rein for a moment, he was sober of mien and taciturn, returning their greetings with a mere touch of his cap. The mare shifted nervously under him but he sat her without noticing, like a somber sea captain in a swell.

They were ready at last. Dermot saluted with his crop, Miss Mims waved, caroling, and the Bentley swept out of the drive.

Hawthorn-drifted, the country basked in a dull glaze of morning sun. They sped over the hedged roads and through the slate-colored villages in a mood of tolerance.

Moira had begun an acid bickering with Dr. Fabret, but J.J., who drove, squinting over his cigar, teased them into a matching of wits, and the others quickly relaxed in laughter; all but Sheilah, who, upright, had gone back to sleep.

"We really ought to show Carlotta the cliffs before we pick up O'Connell," said Fran, and J.J. obligingly took a side road.

"It's a case of stopping or going over the edge of the world," he said, halting the car at the top of a grassy plain, truly emerald green, and they got out and walked to the brink.

The Atlantic, mild and blue and shimmering, lay before them.

It was a place of ultimate beauty and terror. Ranging away like the dark wings of a stage, dark yet luminous with the reflected light of the sea, the cliffs dropped hundreds of feet to the foaming rocks below. Carlotta stood well back from the unguarded edge, her hands pressed to her cheeks. The cliffs were alive with gulls, tens of thousands of them nesting on shelves, now and again dropping effortlessly into the luminous air. It was a soundless place that drowned sound, a place of space, of stirring air, of gull's cries absorbed in the blue sea's breathing, the sea's slow heaving against the rocks.

Dr. Fabret touched Carlotta's arm. "The Aran Islands," he cried into the turbulence, and pointed out the inverted saucers of land in the pearly distance. "And there, the mountains of Connemara—the Twelve Bens."

"Look down, Carlotta, look down!" called Moira, at the edge, her hair streaming, her arms and hands spread as if she were about to soar out into the wind. Carlotta paled and turned her head away.

"There's a famous nesting place below," said Fran,

"for some sort of strange bird. But don't look if it makes you sick."

"Darn it, she's a bird watcher, isn't she?" demanded J.J. "She ought to see 'em. Lie down on your stomach, Carlotta. Fabret, you get on one side of her and I'll take the other." In this fashion they crawled forward. ("It's easier to walk," scoffed Moira.) And presently, grasped securely on both sides, Carlotta looked giddily down on a small island, and through her field glasses identified the outlandish red, blue, and yellow bills of puffins.

Moira was the last to leave. Still poised on the edge, her face lifted and her hands clasped behind her like a ship's figurehead, she communed impassively with the sea wind, and when they called to her she lifted her arms as if in a last embrace. In the car again she was silent.

They skirted the southern shore of Galway Bay, the clouds over the Twelve Bens reflecting vertically down the miles of calm blue water, and then they turned into the gates of Conor O'Connell's eighteenth-century manor.

O'Connell himself was standing squirefully in the drive, but all eyes went at once to an antique roadster painted lime yellow with a goblet of Pimm's Cup resting on a fender and a dark-haired, loose-limbed young man leaning nonchalantly beside it.

"The last I heard of you, Tony," said Moira, emerging with the others from the Bentley, "you were at war with the Arts Council in Dublin."

"Our horns are locked still," he said agreeably, and kissed her cheek. He wore with a certain raffish elegance a turtlenecked fisherman's sweater over faded trousers, and a dark Celtic flush tinged his smooth cheekbones. "The weather's drawn me home to Galway. I hoped to do some sailing, but the wind's died on me."

"This is my most presentable cousin, Tony Temple," Moira told the others. And despite their difference in age and coloring they showed a resemblance, particularly in the high-bridged noses and arched brows. "As well," added Moira, "as one of Ireland's most promising architects."

"A dubious compliment," he murmured, and his dark eyes rested briefly on Sheilah Malloy. He was a self-contained young man, at ease in manner and good-humored, yet giving an impression of latent, Old World daredeviltry, more formidable than New World delinquency.

Conor O'Connell, resplendent in red and green checked tweed with cap to match, stepped in, glass in hand, to take charge of introductions, but their attention returned at once to the 1926 Fiat, upon which the young man expounded agreeably. Its name, he told them, among other things, was Albert. O'Connell urged them to join him in a drink, but J.J. said they had better press on. "You won't change your mind, Tony," said O'Connell, "and come with us now?"

"In fact I will," he replied, a hint of a smile in his claret-colored cheeks. "Miss Malloy has consented to trust herself to Albert and me."

How, wondered Carlotta, did young people manage to arrange such matters so expeditiously? And turning, she saw the answer to an earlier question. Sheilah looked at least two inches taller, her little chin raised, her violet eyes brightly focused, her cheeks faintly colored, her pretty figure tensed and distinct at last: Sheilah had come to life.

J.J. glanced doubtfully at Albert, and Tony added, "If you're stopping for oysters at Clarinbridge we'll catch you up at Maam Cross."

"For a lass who was dead on her feet," remarked J.J. as they drove away with O'Connell, "she works fast. You have to hand it to the Malloys."

"The Malloys is it?" sniffed Moira. "There are no flies

on Tony Temple. Mind you, he's settled down a bit since he became twenty-one, but he used to be known as the Hunt Ball Hellion." O'Connell gave a guffaw, and Fran uttered a maternal groan.

"He reminds me," said Carlotta, "of those wonderful, heedless Irishmen who flew in the RAF in World War II."

"That was his father," Moira told her. "He was killed in the Battle of Britain. Poor Constance. She never thought her son would finish the university, let alone find a career for himself on this wretched island."

O'Connell's face underwent a change. "Wretched island indeed! You talk like a bloody Englishman."

An argument followed about the growing prosperity of Ireland, the progress of industry, and the revival of the arts, ending as most such arguments do with the Power of the Church, which lasted all the way to Clarinbridge and beyond to Galway City, and which J.J., a walking filing cabinet for information, fanned to life when it showed signs of burning out.

And all the while Carlotta sat lost in the unfolding scene. The stoney region out of Galway gave way to the sea again and they drove now straight into the wind which streaked the dark waters of the inlets, and the light had changed, shining brassily as if at an unnatural angle and gilding the mustard-colored seaweed strung out upon the waters.

"For a thousand years," Moira was complaining with a singsong bitterness, "the Fenns have given their blood for Ireland, and even with Dermot selling off the horses one by one the demesne is a lost cause, and no doubt when Aunt Augusta dies it will be sold to Americans and made into an hotel, and that, too, I suppose is progress. . . ."

They turned north into the brown bog country where lonely swans floated on silvered ponds and the Twelve Bens, spotted mauve with cloud-shadow and sparkling with quartz, loomed before them. They passed men ankle deep in dark bog water, cutting peat in neat cakes like chocolate fudge. *O Ireland, Ireland,* Carlotta crooned quietly and gratefully within herself.

At Maam Cross where the roads of Connemara convene they met the lime-yellow Fiat and the flushed and wind-blown young people, and single file they proceeded on into Joyce's Country, the high moorland between the Bens.

"This is it!" cried Fran at last, and J.J. halted the car in a wide pass, with a stream high up on one side of the road and a lake farther down on the other.

They stepped out, stretching, into the pure, high sun and air, warm and wild. Clouds traveled the sky and the flanks of the Bens, bare and moss green and glittering, sheltered them. This was the heart of Connemara.

"It sets free the spirit, does it not?" said O'Connell.

"Oh," cried Carlotta, unable to restrain herself any longer, "I feel like running—flying!"

"Fly, then," said Moira. "Otherwise you might sink out of sight."

"What, here? In this green grass?"

"It is bog. Many's the unwary soul who's been claimed by the bogs of Connacht." Moira's eyes smiled yellow in the strong sunlight. She slid a proprietary arm through O'Connell's and moved him away.

Sobered, Carlotta gazed down the pass. Just when one waxed most sentimental over this lovely island, one struck upon the anguish beneath its surface. She remembered reading that whole companies of soldiers had perished in the bogs. It wasn't fifty years since the persecutions ended, and not much longer since the massacres and burnings, and one had to remember that here in the lyrical West Country the Famine had taken its heaviest toll. For centuries suffering had been as much a part of the land as the bogs. And it was this sense of invisible tragedy that gave

51

the country its richness, its underlying darkness, the haunting sadness carried on the wind.

"One has only to have the mystic feeling," said Dr. Fabret at her elbow, "to hear an ancient chorus." She turned, surprised, and gave him a grateful smile.

They were spreading rugs and setting out hampers by the stream, in the shelter of an abandoned shepherd's hut, and O'Connell had put the wine to chill in the tumbling water.

There was a moment out of all time, Carlotta thought, when picnickers disposed themselves harmoniously about an unfrequented place. For that moment the place was inhabited, given and giving a reciprocal charm, and for that stationary moment the half-reclining figures seemed fixed forever in grace and even their random words indelible. Within an hour or so the rugs would have been taken up, the hampers repacked, the figures risen and departed, never again to return, and not a trace would be left of their visitation, as if it had never happened. With a sense of wonder, Carlotta cherished the fleeting reality, the beauty, of the present.

Tony and Sheilah were the first to rise, and they strolled off up the road, their shoulders almost touching and Sheilah's flute-like laughter floating behind them. With a practiced gravity Tony had set himself to entertain her, and whereas at first her laughter spurred him on to wilder nonsense, in time he paused to listen to it, to study the purity of her face, and he began to wear a broody look of awe.

Fran and J.J. set off in the opposite direction, and Moira, who never made any pretense of her disdain for Dr. Fabret, impulsively seized his arm. "Come," she said. "Carlotta's sketching and O'Connell's asleep with his mouth open. There's nothing for us but to walk, too. Up with you, man." And away they went.

"Ha!" cried O'Connell, coming to with a start. "Oh! Ha! Where's everybody got to?"

"Lie down again, you're in my sketch." She was perched on the doorsill of the shepherd's hut. "They've gone for walks."

"Ha!" O'Connell clapped his brow and sank back again. "This is what picnics always do to me." He lighted a cigarette and gazed up at the clouds. "You're a sensitive being," he said abruptly, without any brogue at all. "What do you make of the Kilraven setup?"

"Complicated," she said.

He grinned. "I like you, Carlotta Fleet."

"I like you, Conor O'Connell, when you don't feel you have to impress me."

He turned his head to her. "That's what I like about you. I don't feel I have to impress you."

"But people whom you don't have to impress bore you, don't they?"

"Leave off. It's too peaceful here for sophistry. I'm glad the others have taken themselves off. You are restful." She gave him a quizzical look. "You are no doubt aware that Moira, that barely civilized Irish temptress, is using me to rouse her husband's jealousy."

"I'm much more aware that you are using me to rouse hers."

He smiled again. "Complicated is the word."

"Conor, will you tell me something?" She put aside her sketch pad and folded her arms about her knees. "Will you tell me about the Kilraven heir who was killed?"

"I'll tell you the little I know."

"His name, first of all."

"Michael Donal Fenn. A kind of Hamlet, I gather, compared to his warrior ancestors. Dermot is the one who takes after them, really; he should have been the heir—everyone agrees on that. D'you suppose he thinks so, too?

Well, this is what I've pieced together from country gossip and what little Moira has let fall." He drew on his cigarette and blew smoke toward the clouds. The voices of the stream muttered and warbled, but all except the near sounds were lost in the open expanse of air and moorland around them.

"Whether he was a true artist or an aristocratic dilettante, I don't know. I suspect the latter. He played the piano well, he painted a little, he wrote. His mother must have thought him a genius, and his father must have thought him a queer. He went to Eton and Oxford, which is standard procedure for the Fenns ever since they were Protestantized and tamed by Henry the Eighth. But after his father's death he went on to Paris to study, which angered his mother. Then, even more against her wishes, he married a Frenchwoman some years older than himself. And so there was one of those unhappy estrangements and he never went back to Kilraven. Some years later, when he must have been in his late thirties, he and his wife were driving fast along one of those straight, tree-lined, French roads, and blew a tire, or lost control somehow, and both of them were killed outright."

Carlotta let her breath out in a sigh.

"No, wait," O'Connell continued. "He lingered a while. The driver in an accident usually gets the better deal, doesn't he? But only a little while. I remember Moira saying, 'Everything was done for him that could be done and more.' And then he was gone." They were silent again for a moment, and O'Connell added, "The story lacks pathos, don't you think? I wonder why."

"You've left emotions out of it."

"It was a needless estrangement and a needless death."

She felt a cooling in her cheeks as if the color were leaving them, and a sad lassitude suffused her body. "They've made a ghost of him."

54

"Blast that tiresome ghost! Let us at least give them credit for not inventing it. Surely it was dreamed up by one of their more fanciful American guests."

"Oh, yes, surely." The dizzying sensation passed, she drew in her breath and got to her feet. "Would you like to walk, too?"

"No, dear heart, I would not. Besides, it is going to rain. See, the others are returning." Suddenly his brogue was returning also. "And I must have something to take away the taste of wine." He struggled to his feet with grunts and groans and rummaged in a hamper for his bottle of Jameson's. He said suddenly, his craggy face turned aside, "I didn't bore you all that much, did I?"

She turned to him in surprise.

A lamentable thing had happened to O'Connell. Following an impoverished and unrecognized youth he had enjoyed some twenty years of fame. "The laughter, the tenderness, the tears evoked by Conor O'Connell uphold the claim that he is perhaps the greatest Irish-American writer of his time." (How O'Connell had resented that *perhaps!*) Then his writing had leveled off, dwindled; he had lapsed into a slightly higher than middle bracket of esteem, and a whole generation had come on the scene who had scarcely heard of him. It remained for him to be rediscovered, but that might not come about in his lifetime.

"I was fascinated," said Carlotta simply, and was touched by the immediate brightening of his face.

A wind swept down the pass then, carrying with it drops of rain, and the peaks had vanished in the mist. The others came rushing up, pell-mell, to gather the picnic things. There were hasty farewells on the road. It was agreed that O'Connell should go home in the Fiat, while Sheila returned with her parents. Scarcely a word or a look passed between the young people; charming and self-possessed, Tony shook hands, and Sheilah, her lids, her very cheekbones dreamy, climbed into the Bentley. They were so restrained, in fact, that Carlotta was certain they had arranged another meeting.

O'Connell thrust his head in the car window, his shoulders pelted with rain. "I'll ring you up, Carlotta. Remember our pilgrimage to Drumcliffe!" His glance darted to the corner where Moira huddled with her arms folded, her eyes shut, as if exhausted by a day of congeniality. "Goodbye all, and God bless! Pray for me on my homeward journey in this ridiculous heap!"

"Love-love," said Sheilah softly, her last utterance for the remainder of the afternoon.

4

Kilraven Castle had a number of new guests. A party of gay, blue-haired, well-to-do widows filled the halls with their penetrating Midwestern accents, and an attractive young family from Virginia came in on the early plane. An Englishman and his wife, the former a Group Captain with a large florid face and red mustachios that curled up on the ends, had arrived by car the night before. The laughter of the carefree widows was infectious and the Group Captain's intense masculinity invigorating, and the atmosphere became suddenly quite festive.

Carlotta went off to paint the cliffs, adding from memory a figure standing at the edge with her hands clasped behind her and her hair streaming.

"That's Moira, to be sure," said Lady Kilraven. "How like her, flirting with danger." Carlotta had found the old lady having tea in the library with Miss Mims and Dr. Fabret. Everyone else was off sightseeing; everyone but Sheilah, whom Carlotta had encountered a moment before in the drive, leaning against the lime-yellow Fiat and engaged in flippant conversation with the personable Tony Temple.

"Yes," continued Lady Kilraven, "you've caught the dark drama of the cliffs." Frequently she uttered a phrase which Carlotta found herself entering in her mind as if in a notebook. "But it's not a disturbing picture, do you think, Dr. Fabret?"

Dr. Fabret, looking sleepy and sage, his head tilted back against the sofa cushions, said no, he thought stimulating was more the word.

"Don't you think it very good, Millicent?" insisted Lady Kilraven.

Miss Mims, knitting as usual on the other side of the hearth, obediently looked up. "Charming!" she sang at once, almost too readily. "I *do* like it!" So often she gave the impression, beneath her enthusiasm, of grinding her teeth. "We'd no *idea* you were so clever, Mrs. Fleet."

"I can almost smell the sea," mused Lady Kilraven. "It's a long time since I've been able to visit the cliffs. This sketch might almost lure me into going there." Her eyes, heavy and clear as glass, lifted to Carlotta's face and for a moment they were full of conjecture. The room around them, insulated by its walls of books, was very still. The tiny fire whispered, a clock ticked. "Yes," said Lady Kilraven at last, softly, as if thinking aloud, "you are in a way an emissary." Miss Mims vigorously knitted on.

Carlotta glanced for some support at Dr. Fabret, but he appeared to be asleep. The room seemed full of intimations she couldn't fathom, she was the focus of an attention she didn't understand, and once again she had the sensation of being guided into an unexplained role. "That may be," she said coloring slightly, "but I'm a weary one. I'll go up now." And she held out her hand for the sketch.

"Of course." Lady Kilraven returned it. "If there is anything we can do, Mrs. Fleet, to make you more comfortable, you mustn't fail to let us know." This time she ignored Miss Mims's noncollaborative silence. "And I almost forgot—Moira sent word inviting you and Dr. Fabret to Rose Cottage this evening for coffee and brandy."

Carlotta thanked her. She was curious, she realized, to see the domestic background of the rather undomesticated Fenns.

Dr. Fabret murmured with a smile, his eyes still half-shut, "Rose Cottage, indeed!"

It was nearly nine o'clock when they set out, but the late spring light lingered and they decided to walk. Beyond the walled garden a lane, or bohreen, fern-bordered, led them away from the castle. The call of a distant cuckoo brought them to a momentary halt. Dr. Fabret, cupping his hands, imitated it, and after an instant's doubtful silence the bird replied, and for a few moments they answered back and forth.

"In the woods behind my house," said Carlotta as they strolled on, "a whippoorwill will be singing."

"Are you homesick so soon?"

"I feel at home here, Dr. Fabret."

"Would you call me Edward?"

"Certainly. And how about you, Edward? You seem thoroughly settled at Kilraven."

"Only for the month of May."

"Your patients must miss you."

"I have no patients as such. I'm a professor in charge of research, a member of the staff of a university hospital. That's why I'm able to take sabbaticals—go off on pedagogic adventures, as you might say."

They had come to the top of a ridge and halted again in the face of the glowing sky, magenta and gold. Plowed fields and orchards in bloom undulated away to a further ridge, where the ruined tower of a bygone century rose above the treetops. A deep and tranquil stream, reflecting the sky, wound through the landscape.

" 'Strings in the earth and air,' " said Dr. Fabret, " 'make music sweet; strings by the river where the willows meet. . . .' Yeats again," he added dryly, in answer to Carlotta's look of surprise.

Hoofbeats sounded behind them and Dermot Fenn rode up on his neurotic mare. He dismounted and walked beside them. At Dr. Fabret's prompting he summarized the farming operations of Kilraven, a complex so all-inclusive, with its herds and flocks, even its trout and pheasant, that Carlotta realized the demesne must at one time have been self-sufficient. For once Dermot omitted his complaint of hard times and sounded merely the detached overseer. His hands continually bowed his crop. "He should have been the heir," O'Connell had said. Perhaps he had to guard his feelings when he described the potentials of Kilraven, straining from his voice any note of devotion.

"Mind the sheepfarts," he warned offhandedly, and the mare tore a jawful of greenery from the bank.

Carlotta kept silent, listening to him, and when his eyes rested on her they were cool, veiled, and uncommunicative.

The bohreen ended at the stream, and as they rounded a willow-draped bend a whitewashed one-and-a-half story dwelling came into view, a television aerial sprouting from its thatched roof. The yard was crowded with spring flowers, and a family of ducks paddled in the sunset-lighted stream.

"Rather a picture post card, isn't it?" Dermot asked Carlotta, with a note of uncertainty.

"Why, it's charming," she told him, also with some uncertainty, for it was not at all the kind of place she expected.

"Would it make a pretty painting, d'ye think?" He was suddenly using the accent, ingratiating and defensive, of the classic Irish Paddy.

"Oh, yes, very pretty." (Too pretty!)

60

"Ye're welcome to try it any time." Then he added with sudden stiffness, "Not that it has the grandeur of a subject like the castle."

She smiled. "I'm not partial to grandeur." Nor was it grandeur, to her way of thinking, that characterized the castle.

"Ye're not," he echoed, unconvinced. But opening the gate he remembered he was host and gave an accommodating half-laugh. "Go in, will ye, what time I'll stable the mare."

As they went up the walk between the rose trees Carlotta's eyes slid to Dr. Fabret; he returned her look owlishly. He missed little through those spectacles, she knew, but if he had organized the contradictions of Dermot Fenn and drawn any conclusions he wasn't revealing them.

Moira, in yellow silk slacks, appeared in the doorway under a yellow bower of roses. "Welcome," she said begrudgingly, with an enigmatic smile, at once enticing. She ushered them into a hallway floored with a depressing linoleum indigenous to the island; boots for all contingencies huddled in a row and coats for all weather hung on pegs. There was a smell of wet dogs. Then she opened a door on the right and they stepped into a drawing room.

No muddied boots set foot on these pale rugs. The windows were hung with taffeta and needlepoint covered the chairs, and the fact that these materials were slightly threadbare made them for some reason all the more patrician. A table draped in blue velvet held a collection, in the European manner, of signed photographs of distinguished personages. Carlotta and Dr. Fabret sank into a silk-covered sofa and Moira poured them coffee from a Georgian service. They expressed their admiration. "Yes, it's sweet, isn't it," she murmured cryptically.

But Carlotta, in her extrasensory way, had an uneasy

feeling. It was indeed a charming room, filled with flowers, it was even a personal room, but it was giving her a peculiar stomach ache.

Dermot joined them presently and offered brandy. Conversation rambled. They touched on racing and the Derby, subjects quickly exhausted due to the ignorance of the visitors, and switched to the Irish theater, exhausted almost as quickly due to the ignorance of their hosts. Dr. Fabret tiresomely got Dermot started on farming again, and Carlotta, turning to Moira, asked for pointers on the Dublin dress designers. Now and then in her discourse Moira threw in an incongruous expression which she could only have picked up from Sheilah Malloy.

How striking she was, curled in a deep chair with one trousered leg tucked under her, her full bosom lifting her silk blouse and her strong brows casting a shadow on her eyes. (Tiger, tiger, burning bright, thought Carlotta unreasoningly.) Her husband perched on a little chair padded in striped satin; he leaned forward, his elbow on his knees. They didn't look at each other or address each other very often, this couple, and when they did they didn't quite meet each other's eyes. Yet it was apparent from the very ease of their bodies that they must enjoy a more than satisfactory sexual relationship. They were childless. Perhaps all they needed, Carlotta speculated, was a less secondary social position—the inheritance, for instance, of Kilraven Castle.

It was their bitterness she felt in their idealized room—their passion and their extenuated love. A cold triviality surrounded them, belittling their latent desperation. Their caged vitality among these faded silks and status-photographs—personages from Never-Never Land—seemed to spell some kind of doom.

As soon as it was politely possible Carlotta rose to say good night. But outside they found a full-blown moon rising over the stream and Dermot insisted they accompany their guests over the ridge.

Inevitably he fell in beside Carlotta, leading the way and outdistancing Moira and Edward Fabret. The path was perfectly clear. When they reached the walled garden he took her elbow and opened the door. "You must see the laburnum tree by moonlight." He drew her hand through his arm and they walked forward slowly, inhaling the cool moon-flowering scents, hushed by the silver and shadow and motionlessness. They stood smiling at the laburnum tree in its loveliness, pale and spellbound.

In the next instant Dermot was kissing her lips softly again and again, little kisses that caught her lips between his, and then his arms, inexorable as oak, strained her closer, his mouth settled in earnest.

Breathless, they broke apart and he caught her forearms to keep her from stumbling. "There now," he told her, his broad impenitent smile flashing in the moonlight, "I've been wanting to kiss you since I first set eyes on you."

She had got her footing and her breath, and she was shocked to find herself on the verge of laughter again. "You're incorrigible, I knew that."

"Ah, but it was sweet, wasn't it, and no harm done."

She couldn't answer, her heartbeat still stifling her, and he led her out of the garden a moment before Moira and Edward came up; he pressed her hand and let her go. "We'll leave you here," he said, "and good night to you." Moira sent a wry glance at Carlotta over her shoulder, and then they vanished into the shadows.

Without thinking about it Carlotta linked arms with Edward and they continued along the walk. She was breathing rapidly, she discovered, and she was now inexplicably close to tears.

"Well?" asked Edward at last.

"Well," she answered, and laughed a little, and a pair of tears spilled out on her cheeks.

"You're really quite happy, aren't you?"

"Why, yes," she said, after a moment's thought. "I suppose I am."

"That's all that matters, isn't it?"

"Yes, that's all that matters."

They were rounding the castle, its crenelated towers silhouetted against the moon-showered sky.

"What a nice person you are," she said.

"And you, Carlotta. Don't forget that. If someone can't help kissing you in the moonlight it means you deserve to be kissed." They had stopped in the drive and he was smiling down at her.

"I don't follow that exactly. And it doesn't sound very Freudian."

"It's not. It's me and thee. It doesn't apply to anybody but thee."

She linked arms with him again. "Edward, I think I need a drink." And they went up the steps.

It was after eleven when she got to her room, and the rest of the household was settling down for the night. Slowly, with the mechanical motions of one emotionally spent, she undressed. She turned off the lights at last and opened her windows wide. The fragrant energy of spring met her again in a flood. Humanity slept, and the real life of the night, the real breathing and ripening, was taking place out of doors, with a transcendant wakefulness. A path of moonlight shimmered on the lake.

Then the music began. It was so soft that she thought at first it was coming from far away. It was Mozart's *Eine Kleine Nachtmusik*, played on a record player, and she realized after an instant that it came from the open window above hers. No one else in the castle could have heard it but herself. She leaned on the sill and listened. Only Mozart had so intimate, so serene a voice; only Mozart offered such tenderness to still the troubled spirit.

When at last it concluded, the silent night took over again, crowding close.

She turned and went to her portfolio and took out the picture of the cliffs. "It's not disturbing, is it?" Lady Kilraven had asked Dr. Fabret, and he had said no, it was stimulating. Quietly Carlotta left her room.

Instead of slipping it under the door of the upper room she knocked, very softly. There was a long silence, and she began to tremble, standing in the dark at the top of the narrow stairs, her stomach knotting with dread. When she could endure the darkness and silence no longer she turned away, thankful the knock hadn't been answered.

The door opened then without a sound. She had a glimpse of moonlight and a pale figure silhouetted against it, close to her, and then the door was shut again and her hands were empty.

Stumbling, her knees almost giving way under her, she groped her way down the stairs.

Miss Mims was waiting at the foot. She was wrapped in a sturdy flannel robe and her teeth were set on edge.

For several seconds they faced each other. Miss Mims's head was quivering and she had difficulty in finding her voice. She swallowed and said at last in a low whisper, "You must not go up there, Mrs. Fleet."

Her solidity, in contrast to the pallid figure above, steadied Carlotta. Or perhaps it was the row of narrow metal curlers across her brow, which accounted for the frizz she wore in the daytime; Carlotta couldn't be afraid of someone wearing the makings of a frizz. "I shall have to hear that," she answered, "from Lady Kilraven."

She knew, and knew that Miss Mims knew, she would not hear it from Lady Kilraven. Lady Kilraven had all but

65

given her permission. What passion consumed Miss Mims, that she must appoint herself the tower's guardian? Even without knowing the answer, Carlotta pitied her.

"You are doing something dangerous," whispered Miss Mims, hissing slightly through her bared teeth. "I am warning you." And she turned and disappeared noiselessly down the hall.

5

It was a relief to be leaving the castle for a day or two. Sheilah and Tony had asked Carlotta to chaperone them to the Aran Islands. "Because," said Sheilah, with the utmost sincerity, "you're rilly a fun-type person." Tony, wincing, shook his head, and gazed at her indulgently.

If it hadn't been for Miss Mims's warning, Carlotta might have packed up and left for good. The sense of being drawn in spite of herself into a labyrinth of family cross-purposes, of being forced, as if fated, to unlock a final mystery, was beginning to tell on her usually amiable disposition. But the prim, jolly, suspicious little Englishwoman brought out an Irish stubbornness in her. And it was this sense of being made to resist that gave her the feeling of being out of harmony with herself; and when Carlotta was out of sorts she was withdrawn, a state Dr. Fabret was quick to notice.

He fell into step with her as she crossed the golden hall, and said, "I hope the weather improves." She gave no answer and her steps didn't slacken. "I'm glad you're going."

She hesitated. "You're glad?"

He smiled. "Yes."

Her face softened. Here was one person who made no demands on her; without knowing each other at all they seemed to understand each other very well, and this was a rare pleasantness. She said impulsively, "I wish you were going with us."

"Do you? That's very flattering. So do I." He accompanied her down the steps and out to her little car where Sheilah waited. The grass and shrubbery seemed washed with a darker green by the gentle rain and offered an ingratiating fragrance. "Enjoy yourself, Carlotta," he said. "You'll be missed." He shut the door of the car on her and briskly retraced his steps.

Sheilah was a refreshing companion for a drive in a spring rain. "I love them madly," she said of her mother and father, "but they're such *characters*. I mean, they rilly don't mean to, but they take over, you know? You're *peaceful*."

"Am I indeed."

"Oh Lord," continued Sheilah, "I hope Mrs. Temple likes me."

"She'll like you." In her prep-school raincoat, with a scarf tied around her radiant, angelic face, Sheilah was exceedingly likeable. They were to spend the night at Rossgharda, Mrs. Temple's home on the outskirts of Galway, before taking the early morning boat to the islands.

"I hope I don't do anything *dumb*."

"Even if you do, they'll like you."

Rossgharda, a brick, Queen Anne edifice of classic proportions, had been a bishop's palace. Tony welcomed them in a wide white hall with two opposite fireplaces, and then conducted them down the rear garden, screened from the courtyard by scalloped, urn-topped walls. He seemed genuinely overjoyed to see them, and kept glancing at the demure Sheilah as if to verify his first impressions. They rounded a house-high hedge of rhododendron and came upon a whitewashed building with a skylight in its steep roof. Tony ushered them into the single lofty room.

A peat fire burned in devout silence and a gaunt priest

68

with white hair dozed in an armchair on a platform. At a call from Tony a high-colored, dark-framed face of great beauty darted out from behind a towering easel. "Oh, you've come, I'm glad!" And divesting herself of brush, rag, and cigarette, Constance Temple came out from behind the easel, wiping her hands on a butler's apron which covered shapeless plum-colored sweater and slacks. "Forgive me, I'm grubby, I'm just finishing Monsignor McDonagh; he's a busy man and I must catch him when I can. How do you do, Mrs. Fleet. How do you do, Sheilah Malloy, and welcome." Her voice was high and airy and sweet-toned. "Oh, child, turn to the light, let me look at you. What a delectable face; no wonder Tony is fond of you. Don't be afraid of me. I am unconventional but understanding. Monsignor, come and meet these charming Americans and you will see why men leave Ireland for the New World."

The old priest stepped down for the platform and gave them a frail hand, his keen innocence adding another dimension to the gathering. "I do see why and I forgive them," he said with a soft, beguiling brogue. "It isn't often that Constance traps me into this vain and passive occupation, but she is a charmer herself and I'm glad she caught me today."

A black kettle steamed over the coals of the fire and Mrs. Temple prepared tea. Monsignor McDonagh engaged Sheilah in conversation on a window seat, making an animated tableau from which Tony had obvious difficulty in tearing his eyes. While the tea steeped Carlotta wandered unobtrusively to the easel. She might have expected something unconventional but understanding, she told herself, but even so the painting took her by surprise.

Without being in any way irreverent it must have broken all the rules of ecclesiastical portraiture. The frail figure with its intelligence and its inherent energy, even a

69

hint of unsuspected disillusionment, was of course recognizable, but the outlines were indistinct. Color was superimposed on color with a palette knife, a vibrant lavender showing through the flesh tones. Moreover, the eye was carried away from the sitter to a window behind him opened to a view of the tranquil sea and a pale green sky, exquisitely brush-painted, and there the eye escaped into infinity. The effect was anything but pious and yet totally spiritual, and Carlotta wondered how the notably dogmatic elders of the Irish hierarchy would take to it.

Mrs. Temple, smoking a cigarette, had come to stand behind her. In an intimate murmur she demanded, "Now what do you think of it?"

"Well, it gives me a most serene feeling. If it were in a gallery I would keep coming back to get more of it."

"That is most heartening."

"You've made us look from the face to the open window. That is the way of faith, isn't it?"

"Ah, now you've said what I wanted to hear." Her eyes, sea-green like her son's, rested on Carlotta. Strands of dark hair fell across her brow, for it was loosely knotted at the back of her head, and the plum color of her costume was becoming to the rich stain in her cheeks. "Do you yourself paint, by chance?"

"A little." Canvasses, their backs to the room, were stacked against the wall. "May I see more of your work sometime?"

"I'm having a show in Dublin soon. Everything worthwhile has gone up to it. I'll send you a notice and hope that you can come. You've already seen an early portrait of mine, no doubt, though I'm anything but proud of it. I was trying so hard to follow the rules in those days. One has to unlearn to paint skillfully, don't you think?"

"What portrait do you mean, Mrs. Temple?"

"At Kilraven, in the dining room. The portrait of

Michael Fenn, the late Lord Kilraven. Tea is ready, come over to the fire."

There was no opportunity to pursue the subject. After tea they all walked through the garden in the fine rain, entered the stately house and were shown to their rooms overlooking the clay-colored bay.

They dined in an oval dining room, its walls covered with mellow eighteenth-century paintings of all sizes, landscapes and still lifes, crowded together frame to frame like a mosaic. Regally costumed and on his best behavior, Conor O'Connell had joined them, and he was pleased to start up his own facetious banter with Monsignor McDonagh and Tony. Sheilah, laughing, relaxed under the proprietary eye of Tony, seemed in spite of her irrepressible slang to have acquired a new dignity. She sat with her spine straight and her elbows tucked in, the pupils of her violet eyes dilated in the candlelight. She was seductive, in fact, without knowing it, perhaps for the first time in her life, and once again Tony's playful, noncommittal expression turned grave and committed.

Monsignor McDonagh blessed them informally at the foot of the curving staircase and retired, and they moved to the firelit library. Tony withdrew to a clinical-looking apparatus—obviously his own invention—for playing records, thereby leaving Sheilah free to chat with his mother, and Carlotta made the rounds of the room with O'Connell, examining the family mementos and sketches, including some of Tony's youthful architectural drawings, which decorated the honey-colored paneling.

"Tony's father and mother?" Carlotta asked, pausing before a photograph. A uniformed young man of splendid dark looks clasped the waist of a laughing, raven-haired girl.

"To be sure. A legend he was in his time."

"And she a legendary beauty?"

"And a direct descendant of the kings of Ireland. Half the countryside was in love with her, and she with her heart given once and for all to Gerald Temple."

A photograph close by showed Tony in hunting costume. "Their son had to be devastating, didn't he?" And then at her feet Carlotta discovered an Irish harp.

"Mother plays it," said Tony, joining them. "She'll sing for us if we ask her."

Rain spattered on the windows behind drawn curtains, and the cone-shaped fire of peat bricks burned golden red. Constance Temple sang to them in a high clear voice without vibrato, passing from one anonymous ballad to another as if she plucked them out of the air. She wore a gown of indigo velvet and a pin of amethysts and diamonds, and with her strong profile bent over the musing harp, her cheeks rose-colored under her dark hair, it wasn't hard to imagine her holding the court of Tara enthralled.

"Deirin de, deirin de,
Ta'n gabhairin oich' amuh san bhbraoch. . . ."

Softly O'Connell translated for Carlotta: "Dereen day, dereen day, the nightjar calls upon the heath, the bittern booms in the reeds beneath. . . ." And Tony, watching Sheilah's enraptured face, wore an expression of such tenderness that it amounted almost to grief.

"Half the countryside was in love with her, and she with her heart given once and for all to Gerald Temple. . . ." The brooding face in the portrait at Kilraven pushed through Carlotta's thoughts. Had Michael Fenn been one of that ardent fifty percent? And who had commissioned the portrait—Michael himself, or his mother? If the beautiful painter's heart had been given once and for all to another, would not Michael have found the prolonged intimacy of sitting for her tormenting? Had that accounted for his scowl? Or had someone else wished to foster their intimacy? And Carlotta considered again the subtly conspiratorial tactics of Lady Kilraven.

"Sheilah droops," said Mrs. Temple, straightening, "and she must arise at dawn."

Tony drew Sheilah to her feet and for an instant stood looking down at her, her hands in his. She tried to smother a yawn, an effort which brought apologetic tears to her eyes. Tony laughed. "Off to bed with you, child!"

"Now, don't forget—" commenced O'Connell, somewhat blurrily bidding Carlotta good night.

"No, no, I shan't," Carlotta assured him. "The flower on the grave!"

And on her way upstairs a final question rose in her mind. Why had Michael left Ireland in the first place?

It was a gray day to begin with, although the rain had stopped, and the sea was calm, gray-green. And forever afterwards the voyage to the islands would come back to them as a kind of gray poetry.

An awe filled them, this comparatively sophisticated trio, when they gazed over the rail at the stone houses on the stone shelf of Innisheer. The Aran men came out from the gray beach hitching their narrow-bladed oars and calling to each other in Irish, wheeling their black *corraghs* over the surface of the clear water, their gaunt faces stained red by the weather, and their pale eyes obsessed with the sea. Staring tourists were transparencies to them or else they were too proud, too obsessed to stare back. The ship's engines had stopped and a dog barked on the beach, its bark distinct yet lost in the quieting predominance of gray sky and water. Some women stood on the sand, their red homespun skirts and shawls whipped by the wind from the Atlantic behind them, on the other side of the island.

Sheilah's rounded jaw fell, her petal-like lips opened to

73

the wind, her eyes filled with an unprecedented respect; she had never beheld a scene, a life, as totally devoid of beautifying and yet as strangely beautiful, as severe, and as moving. Carlotta herself, leaning silently on the rail beside Tony and Sheilah, felt a primitive longing to revert to a dependency on infallible men, to escape the inconceivably complicated and artificial world she inhabited and give herself back to this sterner drama, this simplicity and isolated sanity.

A farewell was taking place on the beach. The women held their shawls to their eyes. A young girl, sixteen or seventeen, with a mop of dark red hair, wearing a thin wine-colored coat, too small for her, and carrying a brown cardboard suitcase, stepped out from among the women, was handed without delay by an Aran man into a waiting *corragh* and rowed out to the ship. The girl sat alone in the prow, facing the island, a white handkerchief pressed alternately to her eyes and held up weakly in goodbye. The word passed quickly from the crew to the handful of ship's passengers: she was taking leave of Innisheer for America.

Sheilah had become agitated, blinking back the mist in her eyes. "She shouldn't, she shouldn't," she whispered.

"Of course she should," Tony told her gently. He wore his fisherman's sweater and smoked a pipe and embodied the philosophical bridge between real and romantic Ireland. "Wouldn't you want to leave this bleak island if you had a chance to see the rest of the world?"

"She'll wish she hadn't," wailed Sheilah, her eyes glued on the approaching *corragh*.

"Is it worse to wish you hadn't done something than to wish you had?"

Sheilah turned to him; all kinds of realizations, reevaluations, were taking place behind that hitherto untroubled brow. "She doesn't know what she's getting into!"

"Of course she doesn't. That's the wonder of it. She has the right to find out."

"In America people have ulcers and nervous breakdowns. Even girls my age."

"On Innisheer they have tuberculosis and everyone's a bit daft." This was not true, but he had made a point. "Would you change places with her?"

"No," said Sheilah after a long pause, gazing at the gray houses, her hands clasped on the rail. "No, but I wish . . . I wish . . ." She couldn't find the words.

"Yes," murmured Tony soberly, staring also at the island. "So do I. So do we all."

The girl had been taken aboard. The ship's engines started up again. The women on shore were already filing back up the beach to their homes, their garments fluttering in the wind. Sheilah clung to the rail, watching the island until the ship had turned and it was behind them. On the starboard side, on the mainland, the Twelve Bens came into view, blue and somber.

They lunched on Innishmore, largest of the three islands, and afterwards Tony and Sheilah explored the ancient fortress of Dun Aengus while Carlotta remained outside to make a quick sketch. They had disappeared, laughing, the young couple, and they came out radiant but serious. Carlotta looked up from her pad. For one brief moment, emerging from a Bronze Age ruin into the ocean wind, they seemed immortal.

Quickly Carlotta painted in the two figures, hand in hand.

It was late when they returned to Kilraven. Sheilah, spent, said "love-love" and tottered off to bed at once. Carlotta, gathering her paraphernalia, field glasses, painting equipment, camera, looked up at the darkened tower. The moon rode behind it in a torn, El Greco sky. Its silent loneliness seemed to wait for her. A shudder fled over her shoulders.

There was a light burning in the library, and as she passed the door Dr. Fabret came out. He was just going up for the night and they mounted the staircase together.

"It was all I could do," he said easily, "not to take you at your word and join you on the Aran boat."

"You do things with such composure. I can't imagine you resisting an inclination like that."

"That's just the kind of inclination I do resist."

"Why?" she asked curiously.

They had paused on the broad landing with its Turkish carpet and cathedral windows. Everyone else had gone to bed and the hall above them was quiet. "That's an interesting question. Because, I think, you tend to romanticize the space you occupy, the place you visit; I mean you render it romantic. While I on the other hand tend to alienate romance as my natural enemy. I'm an exorciser, don't forget." They smiled. "If I had joined you, I might have been a restraining influence."

"I understand," she told him. "It was considerate of you."

"Well, I didn't really think it out until now. I just resisted. Good night, Carlotta."

"Good night, Edward."

Without unpacking she went to her window and opened it wide. The music commenced almost at once. It was a Mozart piano concerto this time, familiar to Carlotta through her Boston Symphony concerts, although she couldn't name its key. Bach, she thought, could lift one soaringly into communication with God, but Mozart, to use Dr. Fabret's expression, had the lovely, endearing quality of me and thee.

76

She listened for a while at the window. The waning moon shone brightly above the trees. The faintly silvered earth and trees seemed to listen too.

She turned presently, took out the painting of Dun Aengus, left her room and went up the tower stairs.

She knocked, and waited, and heard the music cease. The door opened at last, the figure in the colorless dressing gown stood close to her again.

"Michael?" she asked, gently. "Michael?"

6

The morning was dark with rain again, and after Mary had brought early tea Carlotta decided to forego breakfast and turned over and went back to sleep; something comforted her, warmed her, but she couldn't rouse herself to identify it. . . .

"Hey, you're not sick, are you?" Fran Malloy had knocked and Carlotta dragged herself up on one elbow. It was almost noon.

"Fran, good heavens. I'm glad you waked me. Come in, won't you?"

"I thought Sheilah was the all-time champion sleeper. I just dug her out." She handed Carlotta her bed jacket and hair brush and perched on the end of the bed. She was a reassuring sight on a dull morning, capable, nicely groomed, and friendly. "I left her standing in the middle of the room in her underwear; just standing there. Even when you rouse her and get her on her feet you have to steer her around for a while. I'll go back in a sec' and wind her up again. She'll still be standing there." She folded her arms. "It was good of you to look after them yesterday. I hope it was fun."

"It was fun, and it was beautiful." Slowly Carlotta brushed her hair. "They're very real, those islands, more real than anything I've ever experienced, but after you leave them they seem unreal."

"What I actually wanted to know is, how serious are Sheilah and Tony?"

"Ask them."

Fran grinned. "I can be tactful, too, sometimes." She sobered. "I have a weakness, as you know, for the Irish gentry, but when I think of Sheilah getting involved with one of them I get a hollow feeling. She's only seventeen, and right now she could become anything. I thought of that just now, seeing her standing there in her underwear like the little girl she so recently was. With the right man she could become a lovely woman, a real woman, *all* woman. She's got the makings. Or if she took up with the wrong man or the wrong crowd she could become a tough little tart. She's got the makings for that, too."

"You may be romantic about the Irish gentry but you're realistic enough about your daughter."

"I should hope so. What I mean is, I'd hate for Sheilah to become another Moira. I gather this Tony plays around."

"I gather he's never met anyone quite like Sheilah."

"I can understand that. But what does he *see* in her?"

"Maybe," said Carlotta, trying to suppress a smile, "what you see."

"But I don't see anything yet!"

"Oh, yes you do : innocence. Tony might call it purity."

"Might he? And is that enough? How about the fact that she'll be very well off? Let's face it : rich. Does that influence him?"

"He's not impoverished himself. No, as you say, she's all possibilities now. She showed them quite entrancingly on our trip. I think this may impress him much more."

"Carlotta, I'm going to tell you something, something I've never even told J.J." Fran's honest, freckled, baffled face was at this moment delightful to see. "Truthfully, I don't know how *bright* Sheilah is."

At this Carlotta collapsed in laughter, and Fran had to laugh with her. "Bright like who? Whom?" Carlotta asked at last. "You and me? We've just been around longer. The world is full of people who are merely bright, maybe too full. There are so many bright young people around these days it's tiresome, it's almost frightening. Sheilah with her innocence has something else; she has sweetness, and the makings of something better than brightness and harder to come by, which is wisdom."

"My God, do you really think so?"

"I'm certain of it. In fact it might be easier for someone like Sheilah to be wise than it would for someone who is merely bright."

"Maybe you've got something there." Fran stared at her for a moment. "You're rather wise yourself, you know. You should have had children."

"I wish I had."

"You still could, couldn't you? There I go, on top of saying I could be tactful. Well, you've reassured me somewhat." She got to her feet. "I'll go set Sheilah in motion again and leave you to dress. There's just one thing I forgot to mention: I think she's really in love for the first time."

Carlotta dressed languidly. The rain darkened her room and it was necessary to make up at the towering dressing table by electric light. For some reason she was reluctant to join the other guests, already gathered in the library. Perhaps the weather and too much sleep had drugged her, like Sheilah. Or perhaps it was that she needed solitude to think over the night before, to recall precisely each spoken word.

She studied herself critically just before turning off the lights. She had changed. For one thing, the Irish climate had softened and smoothed her complexion and brought out a deeper sheen in her eyes. But it was the shape, the outlines, that seemed different. Formerly, looking in a mirror, she had seen a familiar collection of features that added up to herself. Now she saw a face, not features, as if the familiar collection had contracted, had composed themselves more tautly to reveal a clarified version of herself, her own innateness. "This is what you ought to look like," Dr. Fred would surely have said. Had Harry ever seen her face like this? A faint pucker of anxiety showed between her brows. She smoothed it away and turned off the lights.

She had just opened her door when she heard the door in the tower softly close above her and the sound of footsteps hurrying down the stairs. She drew back quickly and pushed the door almost shut. It wasn't so much that she wished to hide herself as that she knew instinctively the other person would not wish to be seen. The person hesitated before stepping into the corridor, undoubtedly to see if the coast were clear; then the footsteps hurried away. Unable to stop herself, her pent-up breath nearly suffocating her, she opened the door a crack and peeped out. A figure was just turning the corner in the gloom, but he was easily recognizable. It was Dr. Fabret.

The light-hearted widows made a great deal of laughter at lunch, largely provoked by the twitting of Group Captain A. H. V. Gresham-Smith, whose teeth flashed under his red mustache. Fran sat at the head of the table. Lady Kilraven was resting, Miss Mims, beaming, had told them, before withdrawing to join her mistress; oh, nothing serious—just a little overtired. So everyone had an extra cocktail, and the rain, which was keeping them at home, made them feel cozy, and after lunch most of them drifted off for a nap.

Carlotta put on her hooded raincoat and went out to walk in the park. Without thinking about it she had chosen the side of the castle farthest removed from Dermot Fenn's territory. In fact she had fairly successfully dismissed from her consciousness the episode in the walled garden, for the feminine reason that if she thought about it at all it would acquire significance. The distant whinny of a horse, it was true, could quicken her pulse, to her annoyance, but she controlled it almost at once.

It wasn't so much raining now as heavily misting, and the scents of wet earth and shrubbery cleared her mind, and she was soon deep among the spreading branches of the beech grove. Her steps slowed. At last she felt alone.

"Michael?" she had asked, her heart in her throat.

But he had never answered to this name. He drew back at once and tried to shut the door, and she had asked again, softly, "Michael?" Through the open window behind him a box of moonlight tipped into the room, and his face was in shadow, the rest of the room in darkness.

For a long moment he hesitated in the doorway, the sleeves of his robe trembling, his chest rising and falling quickly with his shortened breath, and Carlotta waited, a warm and certain patience flooding her veins, her hand on the outer handle of the door lightly matching the pressure of his hand inside. This was what calmed her; what she hadn't expected: he was more afraid of her than she was of him.

"We've been to the Aran Islands," she told him. "There wasn't much time, but I made you a sketch of Dun Aengus."

He took the sketch from her hand and breathed his first words. "Thank you." He held the stiff paper just as she had given it to him and his other hand still guarded the door.

82

"My name is Carlotta," she told him, words coming to her at random from the calm inner source which was intuition. There was another pause. "I've always loved Mozart." And still another. "He meant to please us, didn't he? As if he said, 'Listen, I have this treasure which I must share with you.'" She smiled. "If you don't want to talk I'd better go down."

His hand shot out from the door and he took hold of her wrist, his fingers cool and adamant.

She said, "I shan't tell anyone I've spoken to you."

He uttered a sentence then, hurriedly, in a breathy rattle, but even so there was a vestige in his voice, a disembodied echo, of Irish grace. "You can't see me, can you?"

"No, I can't. The moonlight is behind you. Can you see me?"

But again he wouldn't answer. His hand still detained her, gripping her wrist with a steady, willful pressure.

"Do my pictures please you?"

He considered a long time. "Yes," he said finally. "Yes. Thank you."

"I will keep on bringing them to you, but you will give them back to me, won't you?" His silence said *No* very clearly. "I come from America, you see, and I shall want to look at them after I've—when I'm home again." Swiftly he released her and all but closed the door on her, then opened it again and took her wrist in an even tighter grip, the bones of his fingers biting her flesh.

"Don't go," he said.

She put her hand over his. "It has been a long day full of sun and sea air and I'm very tired." His hold on her wrist tightened with an almost arch perversity and she sensed danger without being frightened. "I'll come again tomorrow night if you want me to. Good night, Michael."

And presently his hand slid out from under hers, and he stepped back without speaking, and the door closed.

She had arrived at the little temple in the clearing, and just then as so often happens in Ireland the mists parted overhead, revealing mountains of white cloud and an area of sky of the most intense blue, and the sun poured through and the enclosure was instantly hot as a steam bath and millions of glittering drops became prisms of light, and then slowly the mists closed again; the light dulled. Carlotta wasn't a person who enjoyed secrecy or felt in the least comfortable in a plot, and it had been her real purpose in seeking solitude to examine her conscience. Should she, she had come her to ask herself, obey Miss Mims's warning? And Dr. Fabret's warning too, for that matter?

She stood staring blindly at the temple, bereft of its living nymph. There was some ugliness, if not something sinister, in the atmosphere surrounding the tower; did she feel, as perhaps Lady Kilraven meant her to feel, that she was the very person to penetrate this atmosphere? Bemused and becharmed as she had been since her arrival, was she involving herself in a situation beyond her capabilities, one moreover in which she would have to be furtive?

Intuition was as strong, as persuasive and incontrovertible in Carlotta as it was formless and irrational. "Let's wait and see," she would say to Harry, or "Let's play it by ear," a policy which he, who liked coming to grips with facts, had found utterly maddening, as if he danced attendance on a reluctant oracle. Most maddening of all, it eventually produced sound results. Intuition had driven her to deliver her paintings to the lonely man who played Mozart out the window, and it told her now it would have nothing to do with conscience. If you listen to conscience, it told her, you cancel me out; you'll end up turning deaf ears to a really urgent appeal, which would be a sin of omission you'd regret all your life. At least, intuition urged her, trust me a little longer.

She sighed, frowning. If only the man had chosen Tschaikovsky, for instance, whom she found resistible, or even Brahms!

She turned and went back to the castle.

Everyone was up and eating again, crowded into the library for tea, but perhaps it was the persistent rain that quieted them. The carefree widows laughed less boisterously, the family from Virginia communicated among themselves in murmurs. Group Captain A.H.V. Gresham-Smith seemed not fully roused from his nap, and his lady, a self-obliterating little woman to begin with, occupied herself with the London *Illustrated News* and smiled a private smile. Dr. Fabret sipped his tea in a secluded corner, a book face down over his knee.

Or perhaps it was the presence of Lady Kilraven that subdued them. It had obviously cost her an effort to put in an appearance; huddled close to the fire, she looked gray and inert. How long, Carlotta wondered, could she continue to run an establishment like this? Again and again the heavy blue eyes came to rest on Carlotta. And when, if ever, Carlotta wondered too, would Lady Kilraven speak out to her, reveal those secret speculations? Crouched warily just behind Lady Kilraven's wheel chair, Miss Mims knitted away; it was a rose-colored sweater she was making, with odd, intricate knobs down its front.

Conversation rambled on pleasantly around them, teacups clinked, and everyone was thankful to be dry and warm indoors. "Did you enjoy your evening at Rossgharda?"

It was Lady Kilraven addressing Carlotta as if out of a

trance. "Very much indeed," Carlotta answered. "In fact, it was unforgettable."

"Oh?" Some spark of energy seemed to rouse the old lady. "And what made it so?"

There was a challenging note in Lady Kilraven's question and once again, almost unbeknownst to her, intuition led Carlotta on. "Mrs. Temple made it so. We had tea in her studio and after dinner she sang for us. She is remarkable, isn't she?"

The flying knitting needles broke their rhythm for a split second, and Lady Kilraven's eyes came out of their heaviness into icy focus. "Remarkable?" she snapped. "Or unaccountable?" Miss Mims shot at Carlotta a glance of triumph : she had blundered.

"Oh, it's the same thing," said Carlotta, undaunted, although aware they were holding a private conversation in public. What was Lady Kilraven to Constance Temple, and Constance Temple to her? "That's part of her fascination."

"So you've fallen under her spell."

"Was there any reason not to?"

Lady Kilraven's chest gave a start as if she had made a silent "Hmph!" and the passage of words came to an abrupt end. Her eyes seemed to retract, although for a moment they remained fixed on Carlotta with a hint of respect. She looked peevish. Perhaps she realized she couldn't retort without going too far. She lifted a misshapen hand and Miss Mims leapt to her feet; with a curt nod to the group in general she allowed herself to be wheeled away. Group Captain Gresham-Smith, rousing himself, took her departure as a signal to mix a drink at the bar tray.

Carlotta was recalling her first impression of Lady Kilraven, the company parting in the golden hall to make way for her, and how everything which seemed confused and alien from Carlotta's nauseated point of view there-upon took its proper place under the command of that approaching figure. Command! Was this the clue to the character of Lady Kilraven, the life force that bound and balanced her complexities? Had she commanded the portrait in the dining room? Had she been unable to command Constance, legendary beauty and direct descendant of kings, to fall in love with her son?

At dinner Lady Kilraven put her charm to work. She couldn't apologize to Carlotta for something she hadn't exactly said, but she had obviously reconsidered her behavior. Carlotta was half-prepared for this onslaught of flattery and took it with a grain of salt. She studied the older woman and her pain-ennobled face and wondered if she felt pity for her or admiration, or if her feelings for her were becoming tainted with dread, the first intimations of alarm. It was always dismaying to discover the unmistakable signs of ruthlessness in a person of charm and courage, to discover the outlines of a will of such magnitude that it had to be disguised.

Miss Mims's role in the tower's enigma diminished in Carlotta's comprehension to that of small watchdog. It was the shrunken woman in the wheel chair who dominated all, tower, castle, and demesne, and the lives of their inhabitants.

Carlotta lay on her bed fully dressed, but there wasn't a sound from overhead. She fell asleep, strangely fatigued by the inactive day. It was long after midnight when she awoke and heard music at last.

Like a sleepwalker she rose and softly left her room. At the top of the stairs she could hear the music through the heavy door, but it ceased after her knock and a moment later the door opened. They were in almost total darkness, yet the cool hand found her wrist unerringly, and she was further surprised by the authority in the voice that said quietly, "Come in, please."

He guided her into the room and drew a chair to the back of her knees. "Please sit down." She sat down and the hand freed her wrist, and she heard him move away and seat himself nearby. He surprised her again by saying, "It's good of you to come." There was a primness in his thin voice, a slight lisp, like that of someone remembering his best manners.

She said, "You're not afraid of me any more."

There was a little silence, and then he told her unrevealingly, "No."

She was able to make out the window beyond which the moon dimly illuminated the mist. She asked, "Why do you prefer darkness, Michael?" But he chose not to answer. The silences between them were not uncomfortable; punctuated once more with patience, they were more passages of time than absence of communication.

He said at length, and she heard again the lost trace of a more robust Irishness, "I do not want you to be afraid of me."

"I'm not," she told him.

"That is remarkable."

"Why, Michael?" Again he refused an answer. "Haven't you wanted to frighten people?"

"No!" His answer was immediate, projected by a little gasp. He steadied his voice and said again, reasonably, "No, I have not."

"You *have* frightened people, Michael, roaming about at night dressed in white; you must know that." He was silent. "You don't answer to your name."

He said matter-of-factly, "I have no name."

Carlotta realized she was bent forward, her ankles clenched together and her feet on tiptoe, and there was perspiration in the hands tightly clasped on her knees.

With a quick sigh she made herself sit back, her shoulders eased. "*I* have a name."

"Yes, I know."

"Of course, I put it on my sketches, didn't I? Please say it."

After an instant's hesitation he said, "Carlotta Fleet."

"There. That makes a great difference."

"Does it? How?"

"It's too impersonal, sitting together in the dark without faces and names. Do you mind if I call you Michael?"

He had risen suddenly and she found his shadow against the pale window. "Call me what you like!" The words seemed torn from the bottom of his throat in agony.

"Forgive me," she said, leaning forward again. "I didn't mean to upset you. I really didn't."

His shadow still blotted the window. "I know," he told her at last, turned away from her. Was there something liquid in the articulation, was it the sound of tears? "You may call me Michael if you like."

"Thank you. Now I won't ask you any more questions."

He considered for a long moment. Then he said as if in wonder, "It's been so long since anyone needed to know my name."

"Well, I must confess, I thought so!" she exclaimed indignantly.

"It does make a difference."

"Of course it does. We're not cut out to be anonymous. We can't deny our names any more than we can deny our souls." There was another silence, peaceful and somewhat exhausted. "Perhaps I had better go down now."

"Yes," he agreed, again surprising her. And then in his prim, pedantic way he said, "I wanted—I hoped, to persuade you tonight that I am perfectly sane."

A cool draft seemed to curl up the back of her neck and quiver down her spine. She got to her feet. "You don't have to persuade me. I think probably you're just a little out of practice with people, that's all."

"Yes." Was there the sound of a smile in his voice? "Possibly. That is a reassuring way of putting it."

She had to laugh then.

"My God," he breathed.

"What is it, Michael?"

"This is the first time I remember hearing anyone laugh in this room."

"That's just the trouble!" she cried. "I don't know why people won't laugh with you, or don't need to identify you, and I'm not asking why, but I think it's a shame, and what's more, I think it's a shame you accept the situation!"

"Carlotta, I should like to—" He sucked in his breath, a poignant, humble sound. "I should like to practice."

She smiled again. "Why, you're making progress already."

"Am I indeed?"

"You are. I suspect you have a real gift of the gab."

He let his breath out in another sigh, a whisper, an intimation, a dread of despair. "I never did have that." Abruptly, remotely, he said, "Good night, Carlotta."

"You had other gifts, didn't you? Don't be discouraged if I say things that disturb you; it's only because I don't understand you very well. Good night, Michael."

He came away from the window and guided her with his cool hand to the door. "You'll come again, won't you?"

"Yes, I'll come again."

He moved behind the door and closed it.

At the foot of the stairs something made her hesitate, and she looked down the length of the corridor. At the far end of it in the shadows a figure stood with arms folded, a stout little figure in a robe. The watchdog was on duty. No word was spoken, for perhaps forty feet divided them, but Carlotta caught the glitter of the round bright eyes and the threat in the tight smile. And then, because Carlotta refused to give way before this stare, the figure turned at last, slowly, and vanished, and Carlotta returned to her room, her heart knocking heavily between her ribs.

7

Mary of the flaming cheeks drew back the curtains. Well and it was a fine day for a christening, was it not?

Carlotta's ear had become attuned to Mary's whispered brogue and as long as she didn't concentrate on any one word she could make out the meaning of the sentence.

Ah yes, continued Mary, unchallenged, 'twas one of Lady Kilraven's rare outings, all the way to Dingle Bay she was after going, and a band would play and there would be speeches and singing, although God knew how with her poor crippled hands milady would smash the champagne, and Mary hoped the cruel sea wind would not blow too hard on her throughout. Carlotta, envisaging some wild Celtic ceremony handed down from pagan days, expressed concern for the baby, and Mary clapped her hands over her heart. Ah, Mother of God, 'twas a boat, not a baby, that was to be christened! A lifeboat presented by the rescue society of which milady was honorary president.

Yes, even though she still looked a bit dawny she had gone off this morning in the grand old limousine with her collapsing wheel chair and dragging along Miss Mims as well who did not care for the sea at all, and she would not be back until tomorrow and had left Mrs. Malloy to be hostess, and Mrs. Malloy had already set everyone to calling her Lady Malloy and ordered a dinner party with dancing afterwards, and the staff was that delighted.

Mary had never gabbled on so, and snatches of song sounded in the halls, and once again a restraint had been lifted. Had Lady Kilraven, taking Miss Mims away with her, foreseen this—commanded it? A strong, clear sun dried the earth, and the guests hurried out to their cars and the castle emptied. Carlotta took the sun and made a sketch of the laburnum tree at the same time, and after lunch Dr. Fabret invited her to join him on a walk.

They inspected the ruined tower, half a mile from the castle. Once a fourteenth-century stronghold of an earlier branch of the Fenn family, its fallen stones were now overgrown with grass and wild flowers, and snarling jackdaws nested in its spiral staircase.

"Irish ruins," said Carlotta, "have a special stillness of their own, don't they? The silence of centuries. A velvety, rain-drenched silence."

"As I have remarked before," said Dr. Fabret, "a very thin barrier divides you from the supernatural."

They crossed the fields to the pheasant hatchery and saw the drab green eggs mothered by domestic hens. They walked on and found themselves on the hill where a few evenings before they had listened to the cuckoo, and here they rested among the buttercups and Queen Anne's lace. Flat on her back, Carlotta watched the fair-weather clouds traveling rapidly across the sky and lacing the sunlight with shadow. It was a good day, she observed aloud idly, for christening a boat.

Once again Edward sat a little behind her, smoking his pipe and thinking his thoughts. She had never known anyone so adaptable to his surroundings, so content to meditate wherever he happened to be. This, she thought, must be the well-adjusted personality. While she, with her sky-bound view, was engaged in banishing from her mind

93

the glimpse of a television aerial beyond the turn of the stream and the disturbance this had caused in her pulse. A lark hovered high above her, feverishly singing his claim to space, no more than a speck against a cloud. It was a time to shed disturbing memories, to lie still and surrender to beneficence.

Moments passed, and then Edward said pensively, "A bug is making a laborious journey over the folds of your skirt."

She sat up and located the wanderer. "An Irish bug by the name of O'Toole," she said. Carefully she removed the bug to the grass and saw him set distractedly off in another direction. The lark had a vision of sky unknown to her, and the bug a vision of earth, and both, she was certain, were real, related and somewhere united in a cosmic consciousness.

"Carlotta, I must talk to you."

She sighed. "Yes, I thought so." The lark was making his descent now, dropping by stages, singing his way.

"I don't want to see you hurt."

"How can I possibly be hurt?"

"And I don't want you to hurt anyone else."

"Your patient, do you mean?"

"Yes. My patient."

"Do you think I could hurt him?"

"Not intentionally."

"And how could I be hurt?"

"I don't know, exactly, and I don't want to sound as if I'm dramatizing. But there are elements—" he hesitated, "that you mustn't involve yourself in, forces that are set against your interference."

"Do you mean Miss Mims, by chance?"

"Oh, Miss Mims is harmless enough."

"I wouldn't be so sure."

"Carlotta, I'm serious."

"So am I."

They didn't speak for a moment. Carlotta had plucked a blossom of Queen Anne's lace and was making a study of it. "How long," asked Edward at length, "have you known Michael was my patient?"

"About as long, I suppose, as you've known I've been going up to see him. I just guessed it, and yesterday I saw you come down from his room."

"It was inevitable, I suppose, and I needn't feel I've broken my pledge to Lady Kilraven."

She threw away the blossom and turned to him. "Edward, what *is* all the mystery? Why has Lady Kilraven pledged you to silence? Why has he hidden, or been hidden, up there so long? Is he suffering from some brain damage, some psychosis?" She was very warm and her voice quivered. "I can't figure it out. On the one hand Lady Kilraven pledges you to secrecy, and on the other she encourages me to enter the forbidden territory. Talk about opposing forces!"

"Yes, you see? You're distressed, you'll never be anything but distressed if you continue to interfere in this. Carlotta, they have brought me here and I am his doctor, they have given him into my care. I ask you not to go up there any more."

Whether because of what he asked, or because it was he who asked it of her, her eyes suddenly misted with tears. "Edward, I don't see how I can promise you that."

He said gently, "I didn't ask you to promise me."

"Don't ask me, then! Edward, he plays Mozart on records out the window. This is how he invites me— entreats me!"

"I know."

"All this secrecy, and everyone knows everything! Has he told you about me?"

"In his way. He seemed happier this morning than I've seen him in a long time."

"Well, then . . . !"

He shook his head patiently. "Carlotta, I beg you to take my word for it: you could do much harm. And you could be harmed. Do you trust me?"

"I trust you." The look in her hazel eyes, turned fully upon him, was almost more than he could withstand, and it silenced him momentarily. She added, "But I trust myself, too."

"Stubborn woman!" he exploded. Perhaps if he hadn't nearly succumbed to her, his exasperation might not now have begun to run away with him. "This is serious, I tell you! This man has a good chance of recovery, of coming out of seclusion and taking his place in the real world again, if he is guided realistically, objectively, without sentiment or mysticism or romanticism!"

"My God, I don't want to guide him! He liked my paintings because they gave him a *look* at the real world, and then he found he wasn't afraid to talk to me and we've had two conversations, that's all! Isn't this healthy, isn't this part of the recovery you're supervising?"

"Stubborn woman, meddlesome woman! You know none of the essentials about him, and what would happen if you knew them and were horrified by them? What will happen when you leave in two or three weeks if he is dependent on you? I'll not have you undo the progress he's made. Damn it, I almost wish you hadn't come here at all!"

She caught her lip in her teeth. "Now *you* are hurting me." She hadn't known he was capable of heated outbursts, or that she could be wounded by him.

"You'll stay away from him, Carlotta? You won't go up to his room again?"

Bewildered, she shook her head. "I don't know! If I

96

gave you my word I might have to break it. I've never had anyone play Mozart out the window to me. How can I shut my ears to something so charming and appealing, to someone as lonely as that?"

He pressed his lips together, got to his feet. He didn't trust himself to say another word. He turned and walked away.

She scrambled up also and caught up with him. "Oh, Edward," she pleaded, tugging at his arm. She felt she could bear the impact of almost anyone's anger but his. He ignored her and strode on, like an intractable schoolmaster, and she dropped behind, infuriated, and cried out childishly, "Oh damn it, Edward, you don't have to be so stuffy!" He vanished in the shrubbery of the bohreen leading back to the castle.

Returning to the brow of the hill she dropped down again and sat glowering at the plowed fields and the stream, her fists on her knees. A little black-faced gull landed among the furrows, a reminder that in Ireland one is never very far from the sea. The scowl left her brow presently, and she rested her chin in her hands, her elbows on her knees. She thought again of Harry who hadn't had a temper to lose, for all that she sometimes vexed and baffled him—whose generosity included the unlimited bounty of his good nature. Her eyes misted again, brimmed over, and two great tears spilled out on her cheeks.

It seemed inevitable that Dermot Fenn should emerge from the wings at this moment, and she was so unsurprised that she watched his approach on his nervous horse without removing her chin from her cupped hands, and he gave her in return his neutral stare.

He reined in and dropped lightly to the ground and knelt on one knee beside her.

"Why this?" he asked, and his finger came to rest

under the tear on her cheek. Behind him the horse backed to the length of the reins and tentatively commenced a circus performance on her hind legs, which Dermot terminated with an indifferent jerk.

She answered merely, "Oh," with chagrin, and dried her cheeks with the hem of her skirt.

"An unlucky day, is it?" he suggested, smiling faintly, looking into her eyes, and she braced herself against the onslaught of his nearness, his workaday odor of horses and much-ironed broadcloth. With an effort at dignity she got to her feet, his hand under her elbow, and then he stood looking down at her with his head tilted and one fist turned perplexedly under on his hip. His blue eyes were warm and dark.

It would have been perfectly reasonable then to allow Dermot to repair the damage done her self-esteem by Edward, but something amusing, almost comical, in his expression, as well as something amusing in the sunlight itself, the gaiety of the breeze bending the wild flowers, made her smile, too, in fact all but laugh suddenly. "Indulgence," she explained, and his lifted eyebrows wrinkled his forehead, "in woebegoneness. I'm glad you came along and put a stop to it."

"Come to the cottage then till I make a cup of tea for you." It was an almost demure invitation, soberly offered.

"Thank you, no. I must get back to the castle." And she did laugh.

"What's funny, Carleen?"

This caressing Hibernian variation of her name threatened her again, but she answered resolutely, "I said, 'I must get back to the castle.' It sounds funny to an American."

"*Wisha*, Americans sound funny to me." He could turn on a brogue more convincing than Conor O'Connell's. "Don't run away from me. I promise not to kiss you, al-

98

though it would be a pleasure entirely and one I think I could make you share with me."

She turned away, her cheeks darkening. "I appreciate your restraint," she said dryly. "No, there are things I must do."

"Americans always have things they must do."

"Are you coming to Lady Malloy's party?"

"Lady Malloy, is it? I'll come if you want me to."

To her own surprise she answered quietly, "I want you to."

It was his turn to flush. "It's settled then. As a matter of fact we've been invited."

"You're supposed to wear your favorite costume."

"Which would mean that I'd come as I am and bring a great stink of horses."

"She cautioned us to use discretion."

"That was wise of her. Moira might come as a Greek statue."

She smiled. "Goodbye for now."

"Goodbye, Carleen." He put out his hand gravely, but in his warm grasp she couldn't meet his eyes.

She left him. In her room she began to pack her bags.

With Fran on his arm, J.J. turned and halted the convivial procession from the library to the dining room. "We want everybody to have a good time," he announced. "But if anyone gets out of line he goes to the dungeon."

The dinner proceeded with seriocomic stateliness. Fran wanted it that way. She was realizing a suppressed desire. She was playing Her Ladyship to the hilt, even refraining from smoking between courses. Her eyes mocked herself, but the set of her lips said that she was going through with it and no one else must mock her.

The blue-haired widows were ablaze with diamond bar pins and dinner rings, and all the ladies had donned their best gowns, but even so the gentlemen outshone them. Conor O'Connell wore a white *bainin* jacket with crimson cummerbund, Tony Temple a brass-buttoned yachting blazer, and Dermot Fenn, startlingly blond and for once aristocratic without question, had come in the scarlet coat with yellow facings of the local hunt. Group Captain A.H.V. Gresham-Smith, his teeth flashing piratically, was the most splendid of all in dress uniform; a chum, he told them offhandedly, had brought it by jet to Shannon that afternoon. Moira commenced a half-hearted flirtation with him which nettled O'Connell, who resorted to chanting in Carlotta's ear the ribald legends of Queen Maeve.

In the candlelight, Moira's topaz eyes had a staring, withdrawn, impervious quality. It didn't occur to Carlotta to wonder, as it did to Dr. Fabret, if she indulged occasionally in sedatives.

The long dining room, balefully gazed upon by Fenns of the past, had never been more festive, and the servants hurried up and down the length of it with champagne.

The end of the drawing room where the French doors opened on the terrace had been cleared for dancing. Tony had brought some very up-to-date records and Dermot had brought some old ones. Sheilah, Boticellian in green chiffon, began to gyrate gracefully with Tony, and soon, whipped into action by the persistent J.J., nearly everyone was dancing. Between records couples spilled out over the moon-shaded lawn or sipped champagne on the balustrade of the terrace, and it wasn't long before they discovered it was possible to dance on the smooth tiles out of doors. A refrain like a pulsation began to beat in Carlotta's brain: I'll never forget this, I'll never forget this.

O'Connell steered her about, breathing heavily, and on his breath were private odors, of tobacco, whisky, and indigestion, in which she unwittingly read the story of his solitude. Group Captain Gresham-Smith swooped her up in mad waltzes, whistling through his teeth, and J.J. bounced her through a fox trot, while the scarlet of Dermot's coat flashed in and out of her vision.

Breathless, she dropped on the balustrade to rest, and J.J. went to fetch her a glass of champagne. Edward was sitting near her with his customary imperturbability. They had been conveniently separated at dinner and had kept their eyes warily disengaged, but now, laughing, she spoke to him for the first time since their quarrel. "Aren't you dancing?"

"Yes," he answered easily. "Would you like to have a go at it?"

"In a moment, after J.J. brings my glass. I've had quite a lot of champagne already, and what I feel is a most unreasonable happiness." Or was it, after all, a more reasonable sadness?

He was studying her collectedly. "It becomes you."

"I shall have a headache in the morning. Oh, Edward, if only you'd ask me to forgive you."

He grinned. "That's easy. Will you forgive me?"

"I will, gladly. But I think you really want me to ask it of you."

He considered. "Yes, probably. But it amounts to the same thing, doesn't it—peacemaking?"

J.J. returned then, and presently, refreshed, she rose, and Edward's arm encircled her lightly.

"Edward, I'm sorry, I am sorry."

"Dear girl, don't be troubled."

"You're still striding away from me."

"No," he said, quite positively. His arm drew her closer.

"Was it what I shouted at you, like a fishwife? About being stuffy? I'm sorry for that, too, I've never done anything like that in my life."

"Haven't you? That's interesting. I'm glad you did it, then."

"Why?"

"I don't like to think of you controlling your temper all your life, and I'm flattered it was me you lost it with. As a matter of fact, I *was* being stuffy."

She had to smile. "Well, withdrawn, perhaps." She was silent a moment, her brow brushing his; she was suddenly quite tired. "You're still withdrawn. The me and thee between us is gone."

"No. Only at cross-purposes."

"So that's it. You don't give in easily, do you?" She stepped back, a little away from him, and looked at him with infinite sobriety. "All right, Edward. I'll do as you asked. I won't see him again."

He caught his breath; he must have realized what this was costing her. "Carlotta—!" he began, reaching for her hands.

But Conor O'Connell swept her up again and whirled her away. The music, one of Tony's newest records, was loud, insistent, hectic, like a frenzy around a cannibal's pot. Sheilah stood vibrating on her heels, her wrists churning, and Tony was trying to follow her. Gresham-Smith was inventing a yet more primitive interpretation with Moira. The widows squealed and wiggled. "Steady, everybody!" shouted J.J., but his voice was lost in the uproar. O'Connell took an ominous grip on Carlotta's shoulders, preparatory to she knew not what, but at that moment Moira, in a hunt ball mood, suddenly yelled like a banshee, and they turned to find her gripping a champagne bottle by the neck and waving it menacingly about her head as if it were a shillelagh.

J.J. bounded forward. "That's enough!" He reached for the bottle. And suddenly everyone froze.

For one appalling instant Moira's eyes glittered and

she smiled with hideous mischief, the bottle poised high above J.J.'s skull, while the steel guitars crashed on.

Edward, Fran, Gresham-Smith, half a dozen people, commenced a leap toward her that ended at once in a little jerk, for it was Dermot who stepped quietly behind her and simply removed the bottle from her hand, saying, "*Yerra*, stop your foolishness," like an indulgent uncle. (There was something practiced in this, Carlotta sensed fleetingly, in his gentle voice and his stealth, just as there had been in Lady Kilraven's reproof the week before, as if they were used to dealing with Moira's violence.)

Moira glanced wildly over her shoulder at Dermot and then she seemed to come out of a trance. Her arm dropped. Laughing, refreshed, she bent and planted a kiss on J.J.'s brow, and turning, she capered away with Gresham-Smith. No one could believe the incident had been anything but playful, and the dance continued.

Carlotta broke away from O'Connell and was beating a retreat toward the drawing room when Dermot caught her wrist and swung her about into his arms. "No you don't," he said. "Not so soon."

He held her close, his cheek against hers, and danced with a natural grace and timing in the conservative box step of the Thirties, but it was an embrace, not a ballroom clasp, and her suddenly bursting heartbeat only seemed to force her to cling to him, her limbs melting into step with him, and she felt herself lost in a distress of yearning, of conflict and leave-taking.

He danced her to the end of the terrace and around the projection of the south tower and onto the grass, and the moonlight itself seemed to still the racket behind them. Both his arms enfolded her now and his lips traveled across her temple. "You shan't go till you've been kissed good night," he murmured, smiling, still dancing slowly, his voice more than usually musical but unhurried and

103

scarcely pausing between words. "You shan't leave me when I've been waiting for you all the evening, did you know that now, watching your pretty eyes and your lovely frock and the beauties within it, and none of those ogling rogues daring to touch you as I do now, oh my sweet Carleen—"

Almost sobbing with sorrow and pent-up anger she lifted her lips helplessly and his arms tightened and he stopped moving at last.

They broke apart moments later and he grasped her at arm's length, astonished, astonished at his own astonishment, his breath shaking. His hands slid downwards to hers, in another instant he would draw her further away from the dancers, and she knew if she were going to leave him at all tonight she must leave him at once.

The night quieted. Carlotta in her bed lay listening to the sound of laughter and farewells coming faintly from the drive, the rise and fall of accelerated engines as cars with standard shifts departed. J.J. had warned he would send everyone home at midnight, and the evening was ending in orderly fashion.

It was after one o'clock when the appeal commenced from upstairs. It was a statement: now night, now peace, come into their own, take over, now begins the real, the inner life, the liberation of troubled spirits, the sensitive and searching spirits. Mozart had said this. The self-isolated spirits, Michael seemed to add, the sick and lost. Carlotta listened in torment, tears spilling into her hair as she tossed her head from side to side.

8

"For I am of Ireland,
  And the holy land of Ireland,
  And Time runs on," cried she.

A red-headed beauty in a pink smock soothed Carlotta's face with pink cream and another crouched at her fingertips, painting them the pale blush of seashells, and around her the hushed voices uttered what is called the most beautiful English in the world, the English of Dublin. In a little while Carlotta would return to the Shelbourne and change for the private opening of Constance Temple's exhibition, but for an hour or so she luxuriated in this feminine oasis and repacked mental souvenirs.

By now she could have held an exhibition of her own from her swollen portfolio, but her avocation had already brought her rewards. Unlike the quickly surfeited vision of most travelers, hers had grown sharper and more receptive in the pursuit of color and composition, so that in her wanderings she had developed a knowledge of the island of special intimacy. Moreover, a sketch pad is a kind of international passport, immediately explaining the lone lady traveler and entitling her to a certain indulgence, even a benign pity, in much the same way that a Roman collar does a poor cleric, and Carlotta was accepted from Cork to Donegal like any free and naturally eccentric soul. Best of all, her occupation offered a social bridge which her Irish kinsmen, ever ready to fall into conversation, were only too happy to cross.

A spinster schoolteacher from an offshore island, whiling away a Sunday on the mainland between Mass and an afternoon funeral, shared Carlotta's sandwiches beside the road and left with her a glimpse of the heart hunger, the terrible starvation of the spirit produced by genteel poverty. "And I have longed to go to America," she told Carlotta with a beautiful lack of bitterness. "'Tis a pleasure indeed to have met a woman who's done something she's always wanted to do." And Carlotta could picture her seaswept island and a long, limitless gray beach . . .

Deep in the hills of Kerry an entire hamlet, twenty-five souls or so, gathered behind Carlotta's shoulder as she worked, gave her strong tea in a whitewashed cottage, produced a shy, barefoot girl with tangled hair and fiery cheeks like a character straight out of Synge, and proudly told Carlotta, "This one's going to Chicago!" The girl was persuaded to play the concertina and the open door framed an incredible view of turquoise fields and lavender hills. "Come back," they told her, "and we'll keep ye a week!"

In County Mayo an aged man, half blind, paused to ask her, "Are ye stopping at the big hotel? Does Paddy Colligan still tend bar there, I wonder? I don't know who y'are but ye're welcome."

But the thing that undermines a solitary traveler even in the most open-hearted country is the gradual loss of his own identity. By the time Carlotta reached Sligo, near Drumcliffe, she was desperate to hear her name spoken, and she sent off a note to Conor O'Connell. He appeared the following day in a red two-seater, wearing his checked knickerbockers and cap to match, and they set off at once on their pilgrimage.

It seemed to her typical of this poet-proud land that

106

ruined castles and cloisters stood unidentified in the middle of pastures or staring blankly out to sea with the wind singing through them, and nothing to say what proud O'Neill or Fitzgerald had defended them; whereas north of Sligo a small government sign by the road pointed to a Victorian church and announced simply: "Yeats' Grave."

"In ancient times," O'Connell reminded her, "the bard shared equal honors with the king."

A fine rain was falling and the churchyard was wet with unmowed grass and wild flowers and dripping trees. They searched out the gravestone and it stilled them to find the object of their pilgrimage so modest, so still itself in modesty; a jam jar at its base held a decayed bouquet. Even the name was abbreviated: W. B. Yeats.

The inscription offered them its message like the enigma of a mirrored face:

> *Cast a cold Eye*
> *On Life, on Death.*
> *Horseman, pass by!*

It was Conor OConnell's first visit, he had confessed. He sat down heavily on the grave's cement frame. The seams and knots of his features made shadows on his skin's pallor, and the drizzle covered his wiry hair with tiny brilliants. He sat with his hands tightly clasped in his lap, and after a moment Carlotta took up the jam jar and left him alone.

She returned later with buttercups and daisies. "He wouldn't mind such humble flowers, would he?" she asked, replacing the jam jar.

O'Connell raised reddened eyes brimming with tears. "He would thank you with a priceless verse." Awkwardly he mopped his eyes and put away his handkerchief, and

Carlotta, feeling all at once sisterly, wanted to put an arm about his shoulders. He said, " 'I must arise and go now, and go to Innisfree.' " And so saying he got to his feet, and to her further surprise crossed himself in the half-negligent way of the devout, and linking arms with her he held her hand over his forearm in the grateful companionship of spent emotion, and they went out past the Celtic cross to his car.

He drove her to Lough Gill, shrouded in mist like a Japanese landscape, and pointed out what he thought must be the lake isle of Innisfree, and then they returned in an increasingly strained silence to the lounge of the Great Southern Hotel. O'Connell could go for some time without alcohol but not indefinitely; a restless tension eventually sucked at his face from the inside, seeming to dry his skin, deepening its lines and hollows. His eyes darted abstractedly and his conversation shrank to monosyllables. But after the first desperate gulp of neat whisky his countenance filled out again, he welcomed back the world and its inhabitants, and exhaled a great, grateful sigh.

"And how are things in Gloccamorra?" she asked him, with a smaller sigh, for she had been wanting all the afternoon to inquire about Kilraven and at the last minute shrank from putting the question directly.

Slyly his eyes narrowed on her. "Is it the castle then or all the admirers you left behind you're after worryin' about?"

"Conor, be serious, please, and not so Irish."

He laughed, far from offended. He was impressive in the drab lounge and he knew it, his barrel chest expanded in a mustard-colored vest, his knickered knees crossed, his large head thrown back Homerically, battered by unknown voyages but indestructible. Other guests glanced toward him respectfully and the child who served as waiter in grease-spotted miniature uniform bowed almost double over him. Conor O'Connell, too, was a bard.

A frown made itself known in his furrowed brow. "You left at a good time. The castle is chock-a-block full of Americans and there'll be no more jolly little parties such as we had two weeks ago till the summer ends."

He continued after a moment, curtailing his brogue with an effort, "But a strange, still air exists there behind the scenes, in spite of the crowd—something vacuum-like about it, or hushed at least, like the hush before thunder. I went over a week ago, Sunday it was, to pay my respects to Lady Kilraven, who's not been well since her return from Dingle Bay. Everyone was out or in retreat except Miss Mims. Lady Kilraven was confined to bed and Miss Mims was red-eyed; perhaps they'd had a row which they do now and then in their perpetual power struggle. The Malloys had gone off to Dublin and the Gresham-Smiths and the whiffle of widows had long since departed. Dr. Fabret was in evidence but engaged in playing desultory tennis with the young son of one of the guests and merely waved his racket at me. He enjoys a certain crypticallity, doesn't he? One sometimes feels put in one's place by him although he hasn't uttered a word. Even Moira, according to Miss Mims, was having one of her spells when she shuts herself up in her room for a week at a time, and Dermot was in a bloody mood. So I asked Miss Mims jokingly if even the ghost was stirring withal, and at that she turned pale as the ghost herself and quietly shut the door in my face." He made a little mock-shudder. "No, it was not a healthy place."

His eye leveled on Carlotta. "Did you take the gaiety away with you? No, seriously, I don't say the place fell apart when you left, but you seem to have had a salutary effect on them. Is that the proper word? No, it's more as if—" He broke off. "Are you cold, my dear? These

109

drafty barracks! Give up on the tea now, for God's sake, and join me in a glass of Irish."

"I will," she said, for she had shuddered in earnest.

He signaled grandly to the tiny waiter. "No," he resumed, "I can only speak for myself where you are concerned. You are evocative. It's not the same of course as *provocative*. You invite a person to bring forth his true self. You evoke trust. The loving will therefore bring forth love, the spiteful, spite, and," his eyes narrowed again mischievously, "the passionate, passion."

"And the crafty, craft," she said, remembering that nothing was secret at Kilraven.

"Ha!" He grinned. "And if you had no sense of humor you would be unbearable. When will you go back to Kilraven?"

The innocuous question had for her the pain of a probing needle. "I'm not going back at all," she answered simply.

The first person she encountered at Constance Temple's exhibition, in a converted Regency house off St. Stephen's Green, was Sheilah Malloy. "Mrs. Fleet!" she exclaimed in her high, childlike voice. "I hardly recognized you—I mean, in a hat and all. You look *simp-ly* d'vine!"

Tony Temple wasn't far behind her. "How marvelous you could come! Mother will be overjoyed to see you." His darkly handsome face wore the excitement compounded of affection, pride, and amusement that the young wear at the rites of their elders. "She's in the other room being photographed with Monsignor McDonagh. You won't be able to see much of the pictures but do look at the people—Mother collects some valuable types. Sheilah," he said, his voice instantly dropping in key, his eyes darkening, too, with the burden of love, and Sheilah's celestial eyes lifted to him with a heart-rending confidence, "look after Mrs. Fleet while I fetch her a drink, there's a dear girl." But they stood perfectly still for an instant as though spellbound. Then tearing his gaze away he turned and vanished in the crowd.

Sheilah's eyes moved to Carlotta. She smiled. She knew she didn't have to offer apology or explanation. She was still less of a girl now, less ethereal, acquiring more density and dignity, and the first signs of a serene radiance which might become the essence of her beauty. "Mrs. Fleet," she asked with a touching candor, "do you think I'm too young to get married?"

Carlotta hesitated. "Sheilah, something tells me I shouldn't answer that."

"No, I guess it wasn't fair to ask you. I was hoping you'd put in a good word for me with Mother and Daddy. They think I'm too young to even be engaged. They want me to go back to the States and think it over."

Again Carlotta hedged. "And what do you think?"

"I think I'd die."

There was a simplicity in her eyes as she uttered this statement that made Carlotta think of Juliet. "Would you like living the rest of your life in Ireland?"

Sheilah gazed blankly about her as if she might as well have been in Zanzibar. "I'd like living the rest of my life anywhere with Tony." Three tiny wrinkles creased her alabaster brow as she bent her mind to expressing herself. "I think two people can make a home anywhere. You wouldn't believe it to look at me, would you, but I really am the homebody type." Carlotta instantly had a vision of Sheilah serenely knitting before a hearth in a Regency drawing room, three beautiful children playing at her feet; no, four . . . "*Ac*-tually," added Sheilah, lapsing with a chaste little grimace into her vernacular, "I don't dig all this sightseeing. I mean, rushing madly around a country for a month and thinking you've seen all there is to see, deciding there's no place like the good old U.S.A."

Then Fran Malloy was hailing Carlotta over several heads, and splendid in feathers and pearls she plowed across the room. "Well, you're a sight for sore eyes! I've *missed* you. J.J.'s playing golf—he always seems to need outdoor exercise when art galleries appear on the agenda. But he'll never forgive me if I don't save him a glimpse of you. You're looking terribly glamorous, by the way. Have dinner with us tonight, won't you? We're at the Russell. We left Kilraven soon after you did." She darted an anxious glance at Sheilah whose face seemed all at once pale and stubborn. "We were getting much too lazy there."

"Mother's being tactful," said Sheilah in a low voice. "It was me refused to stay there another night."

"Sheilah, I asked you *not*—"

"I know, Mother, I'm sorry, but you don't have to tell fibs for me." She turned to Carlotta, and Carlotta found a troubled, haunted expression in the girl's eyes that she had seen once before, and again a chill shivered up her spine as it had in the lounge at Sligo. "I don't know whether it's really a ghost or not," said Sheilah, "but it was all over the place. I'll *never* stay there again."

"Nobody's going to make you," snapped Fran, trying to close the subject.

"Ah," said Carlotta, like a hapless character in an amateur theatrical, "I think I see Constance Temple."

She approached as tranquilly as a swan on a pond. Cigarette in hand, flushed and flattered, she drifted among patrons and artists and a few fidgety sporting types, all crooning the most beautiful English in the world, and at last made her way to Carlotta. "Now this is truly an unexpected pleasure," she said warmly. "You've been traveling, haven't you, and painting? I'd love to see what you've

112

done. I know it's a personal matter with you, but I'd be flattered to look and I'd know you better."

"For that reason I'd like to show you."

"We'll have tea then this week."

A short young man, all but completely disguised in hairy tweeds and heavy beard, had come up in Constance's wake and she introduced him as the Honorable Niall de Boyne, a sculptor from County Antrim in the Six Counties.

"Does that mean," asked Fran, obviously engaged in equating bearded sculptors with Honorables, "that you are English?"

"Quite the contwawy," he replied in deep and muffled tones, having dragged his eyes from Sheilah. "We are Iwish fwom the thirteenth centuwy. The border of Northern Iweland is mewely one of contempowawy statecwaft." His eyes returned to Sheilah, who stared back with the innocence of morbid fascination.

Tony returned then with drinks, a warmish yellow liquid in tiny glasses, and Sheilah at once transferred her gaze, softening unmistakably, to his face where it remained fixed for the rest of the hour. The Honorable Niall sighed and sipped his drink.

"I'm not going to beat around the bush," said Fran unnecessarily. "Your paintings are gorgeous, Constance. I don't know what it is about them but I've never seen anything like them. How long would it take you to paint Sheilah?"

"Oh, weeks and weeks," suggested Tony. "You'd have to leave her here with us." And Sheilah dimpled adorably.

"Whist, now," admonished Constance. "I shan't beat about the bush either. I long to paint this Sheilah Malloy, just as she is, before she grows a minute older."

"That's just what I had in mind," said Fran.

"If you brought Sheilah down tomorrow, perhaps it could be done in two or three weeks' time."

"J.J. has to be in on this. Why don't you join us for dinner? Carlotta's coming." She added hospitably, "And you, too, er—uh—Mr. de Boyne."

"Thank you, I have a pwevious engagement." He drank in a last look at Sheilah, unaware of the undying impression he himself had made. No one in the circle would ever again utter his final words except as he pronounced them. "Much to my wegwet."

The lobby of the Shelbourne Hotel is one of the great crossroads of Ireland. The commotion of human traffic never ceases. Persons bent on every kind of mission, from banker to bookmaker (known locally as turf accountants), stream in and out. Pages bawl names of Gaelic origin. American tourists humbly approach the altar of the omnipotent head porter, and track followers in native tweeds, racing forms under their elbows, prowl restlessly over the marble floor. A senator from the Daill Eireann hurries to a private dinner party, and a film star with his indispensable retinue passes a hawk-faced countess from the hinterlands returning from Phoenix Park. Telephones ring incessantly at the reservations desk and business is brisk at the tobacconist's counter, where sweepstakes tickets sell for a pound.

Carlotta was threading her way through the crowd when her eyes fell upon a figure crossing before her with a certain grace, its legs tightly enclosed in cavalry twill, its torso wearing a somehow endearingly aged jacket, and then she recognized the fair cropped hair of the manager of Kilraven demesne. At almost the same moment the anonymous glance he customarily wore in public moved sideways to discover her, and without changing expression he wheeled and intercepted her.

114

"Carlotta," he acknowledged solemnly, touching her sleeve with his folded newspaper, and his regard passed uneasily over her citified costume and on to the passers-by.

"Well, Dermot," she managed to say, her heart thudding giddily; but she smiled, realizing that in settings foreign to his own he was immensely shy.

His paper tapped her again and he said, still sober of mien, "Come along into the bar with me."

He settled her on a padded banquette, and unlike the imperious O'Connell he worked his way to the crowded bar himself and returned carefully with a drink in each hand, looking unconsciously boyish in the act, and then he crouched beside her. "Well," he murmured, peering into his goblet of Irish and water, "and have you roamed the highways and byways of the island to your satisfaction?" She had forgotten how melodious his voice could be, like a vested privilege he exercised when he chose to.

"I have." What was the point of such heart-fluttering, she asked herself? The moonlit nights of Kilraven were far behind her. She took a reckless swallow from her own goblet and tried to relax. "What brings you to Dublin, Dermot?"

"Business," he told her. He straightened briefly and his blue eyes met hers for the first time with a flicker of amusement, and then he was fingering his goblet again, revolving it on the table top. "Which means trying to sell something," he added, pursing his lips, "namely horses. And where have you come from dressed like a duchess?"

She offered him the catalogue of the exhibition.

"Constance Temple, is it?" he said, immediately reverting to his rustic dialect. Was it the art world that threw him off—dressy private showings, clever small talk? "My late cousin was in love with her, did ye know that?"

"Yes, I gathered so. Were you in love with her, too?"

115

He smiled without lifting his eyes. She had pleased him; this was the kind of talk that relieved his shyness. "Would you be jealous if I told you I was?"

"Try me and see."

Still he didn't look at her, but smiled at his glass. "Well, then, I'll tell you I was not. She is a fine beautiful woman with her head in the clouds, and no one but the heroic Gerald could meet her on such a plane. Michael was a scholar, you know, with his nose to the ground, even when we were children, and she never could take him seriously. I kissed her once or twice."

"Of course," she said fatalistically.

"When I was seven."

"You started young."

He raised his head at last and grinned at her. " 'Tis a lifelong source of enjoyment." She colored, and strangely, his grin faded as he watched her, his brow wrinkled, and he fell to revolving his glass again. She had never seen him make a nervous gesture before. A tiny unconscious sigh of tension escaped him.

"Please don't think me inquisitive——" she began.

"I would not think you inquisitive," he interrupted, and his gravity disturbed her more than his teasing.

"——but is everything all right at Kilraven?"

He glanced at her sideways. "What are you asking?"

"Is Moira well?"

He stiffened. "Who has been gossiping to you?"

"Several people have hinted that—well, that some of you at Kilraven seemed a bit under the weather recently."

"A bit under the weather, is it?" He straightened, folding his knuckles under on his hip pockets. "My aunt is failing. It will be a miracle if she ever gets up again. They have canceled all their reservations, it's that serious. I've left her only to come up to town and scrape up a few

116

pounds for the unending battle against the creditors and rate collectors." There was always a note of bitterness when he sang this complaint, but it rang now with something like anguish. "It isn't for me to shed tears for those who are a bit under the weather."

"I didn't know," she told him. "I hadn't heard any recent news. I'm distressed to hear this about Lady Kilraven!"

"She is an old soldier," he allowed himself to say, and set his mouth grimly.

The jovial hubbub and clatter of the bar filled the silence between them.

Dermot's hand moved suddenly to grip hers. "Is it really you, Carleen, sitting beside me?" His voice was low, grating, and almost begrudging. "I didn't think to see you again, I didn't truly. It is such a blessing, such an unexpected blessing." It was as if the surge of his anger had carried him helplessly without reflux into this wave of tenderness.

("And the passionate, passion," Carlotta recalled, on guard.)

When she didn't answer he let her hand go. "Will you have another drink?" He was uncertain again, avoiding her eye.

"No, I must go up shortly, I'm having dinner with the Malloys. Why don't you come, too? I could call Fran, I know she'd—"

"No; no. I'm dining with some cronies. Though I could get out of it easily enough if you would dine with me. I'll take you to the Gate if you like, and then to a marvelous old pub, and we'll make a tearing gay evening of it."

She smiled, "Thank you, no," she said, although the invitation charmed her.

"Tomorrow, then?" He took her hand again. "Dear

117

God, I know nothing of your plans, how long before you'll be leaving for the States and all of that. Carlotta, one last gala evening?"

She shook her head, and at last she made herself say, "Dermot, I don't trust us."

Once more he relinquished her, and brooded over his glass. He said stubbornly, "I want to see you before you go."

She held out her hand for him to shake. "Goodbye, Dermot."

"Now, is it?"

"Now. Dermot, it's better so."

His handclasp was weightless, his blue eyes leveled on her in a hot stare. "It's just as well, yes. What a mercy you can be so cool-headed!" He uttered the words quietly, incisively, but his voice, even his head, shook with a furious tremor. He replaced her hand firmly in her lap. "Go while the going is good, as they say. As for me, I have enough to contend with without an aching heart and an ache in the groin, so it's a good thing altogether. For once I'm being sensible about a woman."

She was on her feet, her glass overturned, and he rose also. It was a pity, she thought somewhere in an unstunned part of her brain that their last moment together should be filled with this shock and fury. And then, his eyes following her, she left him.

As it turned out she didn't dine with the Malloys. Under her door she found a telephone message: "Please call Dr. Fabret in Room 33 as soon as you come in."

9

In her one Dublin extravagance, a yellow coat of hand-woven wool, Carlotta huddled in her corner. Edward drove her car. It was a rainy morning and the windshield made a plaintive singsong, and they had spoken only a word or two since leaving the Shelbourne.

Constance Temple had telephoned earlier. "We missed you last night," she began in her thin, sweet voice. "Did Fran tell you it's arranged for me to paint Sheilah?"

"Yes, she called this morning. I'm glad about that."

"And so am I. We're all going back to Rossgharda, perhaps Fran told you. Carlotta, I wish you would come, too. Go there direct, today."

"I must go back to Kilraven, Constance."

There was a little pause. "Carlotta, I wish you would not."

"I'm convinced I must."

"May I see you before you go? Now?"

"I'm leaving in twenty minutes with Dr. Fabret."

"All right. I'll not keep you. But then I must tell you at the risk of seeming not to mind my own business that I have a bad feeling about your going. Did you know they have canceled the reservations of all their other guests?"

"Lady Kilraven has had another attack."

"I know that. But I don't like it. Carlotta, I had this feeling once before. It was after Gerald was killed, and

I was finishing Michael's portrait, and although it may sound daft to you, I felt without a shadow of a doubt that I was not safe in that house." There was another pause, and Carlotta heard the echo of her own breathing in the telephone. "I've never been back. Please think it over, and come to Rossgharda if you change your mind."

Still huddled in her bright coat, Carlotta searched in her purse for the gray envelope with the small red crest. The few words it contained, inscribed in a quaking scrawl, seemed frail under the weight of unstated trouble.

My dear Carlotta:

You are missed at Kilraven. It would please me greatly to have you here again. Will you come as my guest for a few days? We will all make you welcome. I have asked Dr. Fabret to deliver this to your hand and to drive you back if you should find it in your kind heart to indulge me.

Augusta Fenn

The road that crosses Ireland from Dublin to Limerick unrolled monotonously, shiny with rain.

"I keep thinking," Carlotta reflected, all at once aloud, "what it must have cost Lady Kilraven to write me this." But Edward kept silent, and she added, "And what it must have cost you to bring it." He conceded her a faint smile. "I wonder why you ever agreed to do it."

"Because she asked me to," he told her. "Because she is very ill."

"There's more to it than that."

"Yes, of course."

He had arranged to meet Carlotta the night before in the mezzanine lounge instead of her room, and from that moment had conducted himself with dignified reserve.

His manner was formal and his youthful face behind his glasses blandly unrevealing; even his upright posture was somehow that of the professional man.

She said resignedly, "You are being very forebearing."

His armor cracked then and he gave a quick breath of a laugh. "How long," he asked, "will you continue to punish me?"

She said, staring at the shiny road, "Edward, let's not fence. You did come for me. I am going back."

"Yes. All right." He administered the brakes, slowed the car and brought it to a halt on the grass beside the road. He turned to her, his arm on the back of the seat behind her. "There's something I want to get straight. I told Lady Kilraven I would not persuade you to go back against your better judgment. We're only an hour from Dublin. It's not too late to turn around."

Why did he sometimes have the effect on her, she wondered, of making her want to cry? "You didn't persuade me. You couldn't have been more impersonal—I understand that now. I'm going back because I can't refuse."

"It may not be pleasant at all."

"It may not be. I'm almost sure it won't be."

He gave a little whistling sigh through his teeth and got the car underway again. "I will help you all I can."

"Edward, I appreciate the awkward position you're in."

"Awkward! It's damn near impossible!"

She smiled. "There, now, you sound much more human. I have a feeling, you know, that if you were to go through life successfully avoiding awkward situations you'd be insufferable."

"Do you now."

"You'd never get to know yourself."

"What insight, Dr. Fleet."

"I mean," she said, undaunted, "embarrassment is good for you."

"You mean it keeps me from getting overly stuffy. Overstuffed, as you might say."

"Exactly. It forces you to recognize a certain amount of youthful uncertainty in yourself. You have precious little, mind you, but that little is very becoming."

"Well, thank God for small favors."

"Smug, perhaps, is a better word than stuffy."

He snorted. "Halfway between stuffy and insufferable."

"Why aren't you married, Edward?"

"Mind your own business."

"Perhaps you've been too easily satisfied with your work. You keep postponing marriage."

"I've been too busy avoiding awkward situations."

"Haven't you even a mistress? Girl friends? What do you do about your libido?"

"What do you do about yours?"

She flushed then unexpectedly; the restrained violence of the mutual-rejection scene the night before in the Horseshoe Bar awoke hotly in her memory and faded again into gray sobriety. Edward glanced at her quizzically and she was silent for a time, and the wet miles unfolded.

"Edward, it's only fair that I know something of what to expect at Kilraven, isn't it?"

"I don't see how anyone can know that."

"Oh, please, please, can't you have done with evasions?"

"Look Carlotta—" he began sharply, and checked himself. "What do you want to know?"

"Tell me what happened after I left."

"My patient suffered a relapse."

The flat statement sent another shudder over her. "As you predicted."

"It was more severe than I predicted."

A little moan escaped her. She said dully after a while, "I don't suppose you could call him Michael, could you, instead of 'my patient'? You couldn't tell me he took to roaming around the castle at night again, dressed in white, instead of saying he had a relapse? Even though it's a fact, it sounds too spooky, doesn't it?"

"Spooky!" he exploded, and laughed in spite of himself.

"Yes, you see, that's the difference between thee and me, as you once pointed out. I use picturesque terms that horrify you, and yet in my own way I call a spade a spade."

"You romanticize, is what I pointed out, and if calling abnormal behavior spooky is your way of calling a spade a spade, that's your privilege. Be fair, Carlotta! He *is* my patient and I must express myself about him professionally."

"Yes, Edward. All right."

"And this difference is not so much between thee and me as in our relationship to Michael. This is what brought about our conflict. You longed to help him while I must work for him to help himself."

"I am emotional about him while you must be objective. Compassion versus dispassion."

"There you go again! Very well, we might as well face it: where Michael is concerned we speak different languages."

"And yet I think we understand each other. And we must have some kind of truce now, mustn't we?"

"My dear Carlotta, having to ask you for a truce is what makes my position so awkward. The smug professional eats crow. No, as a matter of fact there's a great deal to be learned from his response to your return. For one thing, I'm not really sure to what extent he's actually dependent on you."

"Lady Kilraven has invited me for a few days, and I can't let them become an indefinite length of time. What's to prevent your patient having a second relapse when I leave again?"

"Don't think I haven't considered the possibility."

"Oh, God."

"Yes. Moreover I have to consider my own departure. My arrangement with Lady Kilraven was to stay a month and already the time is up. She may have to resign herself to his hospitalization."

"One thing more," Carlotta asked at last. "What about 'the forces set against my interference'?"

"Lady Kilraven wants you back. I think you'll find she'll be much more open with you."

Carlotta sighed. "Somehow that sounds like another of your evasions!"

"I'm sorry," he said quietly. "Trust me."

She turned to him. "You asked me that once before."

"Yes. And I drove you away, didn't I?"

"Trusting you made me go of my own accord. I still trust you."

He was silent for a time. "Sometimes," he told her, more quietly still, "you touch me to the quick." He added presently, "Your trust is an unusual responsibility. I mean that I value it. You have guts, Carlotta." He smiled, rousing himself. "In fact I hold you very dear indeed, even though sometimes I could shake you."

"Why, thank you, Edward." And the depression, which had dogged her ever since the evening before, lifted momentarily. "You're a dear yourself, you know, even though sometimes you make me turn into a fishwife. And now I could do with some strong tea."

124

They lunched in Borris in Ossory, the halfway point, but when they returned to the car he paused, his arm once more behind her on the seat. "It's not too late to turn back to Dublin. I'll gladly do it."

"You're very kind, Edward. You really are." And again her eyes smarted. "I'll go on to Kilraven."

He studied her, smiling a little, and then he bent closer and kissed her gently on the lips and they regarded each other for a moment with pleasant solemnity. The truce was ratified.

They drove on.

The windshield wipers thumped and whined implacably, and Edward smoked his pipe. Carlotta, lulled, suddenly recalled her own world at home in the way that a person fleetingly recalls the fact of his childhood or a visit to a foreign land—her little world of gardening, painting, community projects, a fortnightly jaunt to the Symphony or the theater. She saw herself leaving it behind her with trepidation, conscience-stricken about her flower beds, bent upon a poetic water-coloring tour of the Emerald Isle. She smiled into the collar of her yellow coat. "Who knows," Dr. Fred had told her encouragingly, almost patronizingly as it now seemed, "you might meet with adventure!"

The sky over the castle was a dark marine blue, she decided with her trained eye, and almost without realizing it, she imagined her brush producing on wet paper the lowering folds of cloud, the pale sickly green wash for the lake, and lastly superimposing the battlements in blue-black, leaving blank rectangles for the staring windows. Were there field glasses observing her return? She sat upright, gripping her purse across her lap.

Edward brought the car to a halt before the great

125

stone porch and turned to her searchingly. She didn't trust herself to delay the moment; she opened the car door.

"We will all make you welcome," Lady Kilraven had promised, and Miss Mims opened the inner door with a fixed smile: the smile for welcoming kind callers when there is sickness in the house. Carlotta made no effort to search behind it. Bustling, Miss Mims hurried after her into the golden hall, polished and silent, and the golden dog sauntered forward, wagging his tail. "We've given you your old room," sang Miss Mims. "When you've caught your breath, Lady Kilraven would like to see you. Just ring and Mary will take you to her."

Turning, Carlotta exchanged a glance of *au revoir* with Edward, who stood perfectly still, watching her, and she went up the stairs.

Instead of lilacs there was now a silver bowl of roses on her desk—Peace roses, no less, almost the size of cabbages, and she bent over them for a long moment, breathing their fragrance, and then she rang. Mary, who must have been lurking nearby, knocked almost immediately.

"Oh, I'mthatgladt'seeye Madam," she whispered hoarsely, and buried her face in her apron, giving way to one or two wailing sobs. In the next instant she was laughing, her face uncovered. "Musha, will ye look at me now, and milady's after givin' *sthrict* orders not to worry ye!" She was not so red of cheek as before and her large hands, clasped before her, tugged at the knuckles.

Then with her head bowed again, looking neither to right nor left, she led Carlotta swiftly down the stairs again and into the south wing, and presently after a turn or two they halted at the end of the corridor. Mary knocked. "Ye'llfindherterriblechanged, Madam," she whispered, and scuttled away.

Miss Mims opened the door on a sitting room done in

126

rose damask. "We've been looking forward all day to seeing you," she whispered conspiratorially. "We tire easily, remember—we're not very strong!" And she opened the door into the bedroom.

It was a corner room, overlooking the park in front and the tennis courts at the side. The bed, immense, carved, Victorian, stood between the side windows. Carlotta came to a shocked standstill. Was it possible that in three weeks' time the dominant, indomitable figurehead of Kilraven could have shrunk to this handful of bones and shiny yellow skin? She occupied no more space in the bed than a child of six. The prominent hooded blue eyes moved slowly from some distant vision to rest upon Carlotta and slowly brought her into focus.

Pity and a common, unqualified grief all but closed Carlotta's throat, and she was grateful for Miss Mims's fussy ministrations, placing an armchair by the bed, patting cushions, and murmuring gaily as if launching a juvenile tea party. The crippled hand, its knuckles doubled, lifted from the faded green silk counterpane in an impatient half-motion, and Miss Mims backed away, ("We mustn't talk too long! We need our rest!") and the door closed after her at last.

Carlotta leaned forward in the armchair. "I'm glad you sent for me."

Lady Kilraven's eyes, clear and glassy still, a darker, deeper, more glacial blue than her nephew Dermot's, continued to focus on Carlotta, but for a moment she seemed to be having difficulty marshaling her thoughts. Where her white sagging cheeks had hung there were now sallow concavities, and the eyes and temples were sunken, too, and Carlotta recognized desolately this terminal revelation of skull and understood better why Edward had come for her in Dublin.

"I'm very glad," responded Lady Kilraven at last in

a small, rusty voice, like that of a child with a sore throat, "you came." And there was an innocence, possibly misleading, in the voice now. "Dr. Fabret didn't tell you I was dying, did he?"

Was it to be that kind of interview? She sat back and gripped the arms of her chair. "No, Lady Kilraven, he did not."

"I requested him not to. I have put him to a lot of trouble."

Carlotta, wondering if Lady Kilraven were altogether rational, answered, "I've already told him I think it's good for him."

A little smile flickered in the depths of her heavy eyes. "Yes. One is tempted to discompose him." But her mind quickly relinquished Dr. Fabret and her eyes wandered and then came back to rest on Carlotta with a sharper focus. "I do tire easily. I shall try to come to the point, and—" her child's breast under a creamy silk jacket lifted momentarily in a quick rueful breath, "—to be frank."

There was a pause in which she seemed to collect her strength, and then she asked, "Did you know the day you arrived was my son's birthday?"

Carlotta, still gripping the arms of her chair, shook her head.

"Miss Mims considers it Irish nonsense to make omens out of such coincidences." Lady Kilraven's deformed hand moved restlessly on the counterpane. "So do we all until we need to believe in them. We needed in this household a person of innocent sympathy, someone unburdened by any knowledge of family secrets . . ." Her eyes had moved to the framed sky beyond Carlotta. The light of the rainy afternoon had reached that moment of standstill when it hung steady and white at the windows; in a few moments it would begin to fade.

"You see," Lady Kilraven continued, her lids drooping

128

now, perhaps over thoughts she couldn't entirely reveal, "with the beginning of this illness, the knowledge that my days were numbered, I had to face the fact that I had wronged my son. I had managed badly, very badly. All of his life, Carlotta!" A fine sheen of perspiration had broken out over her yellowed face. "I had driven him from Kilraven, his home, I had refused to recognize his brief happiness abroad, and after his accident it was I who had kept him hidden for so long." Her spine was rigid, and two tiny rivulets, thin as strands of silk, slid unnoticed from the corners of her eyes into the hollowed temples.

But her small scratchy voice continued relentlessly. "It seemed too late to make amends. I had long ago depleted the family resources in the search for medical miracles. And then Dr. Fabret delivered a paper in Dublin which was reported in the newspapers, a paper about his treatment of mental impairment following severe physical injury. He sounded confident, he was young, he was— American. I sought him out."

She was silent for a few moments, lost in thought, or perhaps guarding her strength. For the first time Carlotta saw the effect of the lids closed over the mountainous eyes, the pallid perspiring skin translucent, revealing nets of blue veins. The veil, Carlotta thought, between the complicated functioning of life in this body, and death, was just as fragile.

She spoke again but her eyes remained closed. "He couldn't promise a miracle, of course. He couldn't even promise improvement. Or perhaps it was a miracle that he was willing to give up his vacation and come here for a month."

"A blessing," interposed Carlotta softly.

There wasn't time to acknowledge the difference between miracles and blessings, self-interest and selflessness. Lady Kilraven ignored the interruption. "He was methodical, a man of science. His examination alone took several days. And I was impatient. Do you know that it has been a long time since I have seen my son?"

A little involuntary sound came from Carlotta.

"No. This is the price I have paid. My grief for him— yes, even my shame—made me encourage him in shutting himself off from the world. He has shut me out, too." Her eyes opened and she said, bleakly bringing out each word without cadence, "I do not expect ever to see him again."

"Oh, but perhaps now—" Carlotta gasped.

"It doesn't matter now. This was not the miracle I looked for. It isn't to me I wish him to return, but to life itself. He is, after all, the heir to Kilraven, the Lord Kilraven. I wish to die knowing he will be the man he was intended to be."

Her lids drooped, her hands were still. She was tiring. "Let me finish. I didn't know what more was needed besides Dr. Fabret's skill, but his very skill seemed to me lacking in promise. Perhaps I looked for a naïve, unprofessional show of optimism." She paused a moment. "And then you came."

The corners of her lips spread slightly. "You appeared out of the blue, unannounced, on my son's birthday, with the naïveté, the optimism, the sympathy, ready-made in your face. I felt you hadn't come for nothing, and very soon I came to believe you could supply what Dr. Fabret could not, and between the two of you there was a chance of success. For the first time I felt hope."

There was another silence, the lids closed again. Carlotta realized she had mixed feelings. There was something not altogether gratifying in being taken for an omen, a fortuitous instrument of fate in answer to another's conscience-stricken need. And she had, too, a sense

130

of cloudiness, of not yet getting to the heart of the matter. *Why?* she had asked subconsciously half a dozen times during Lady Kilraven's recital. Lady Kilraven had told her little, in fact, that she didn't already know. She had an indefinable feeling that they were still beating about the bush.

But, as if in answer to these misgivings, Lady Kilraven said, "I owe you this much of an explanation." Her voice had faded to a hoarse whisper and a frown squeezed her waxen brow in a row of tiny wrinkles. "In a sense I must explain why I cannot explain anything further. You acted spontaneously when you came here, out of a natural kindness of heart, as it was important for you to do, for this is what Michael responded to, and it is important for you to do so again. There may be great unpleasantness in store for you, but I think you must realize that, and I would not be showing respect for your kindness were I to prepare you for this unpleasantness. Carlotta, believe me, it is not easy to hold back the truth from you. Whatever you may think of me, someday you will honor my faith in you." Her eyes were fixed imploringly on Carlotta, and once again Carlotta's misgivings were lost in pity.

"You have come back," whispered Lady Kilraven at last, "and I am grateful." Her lids dropped suddenly in exhaustion, and Carlotta rose.

Baffled, sorrowing, she bent and touched the old woman's arm, no more than a tube of bone under the silk sleeve. "I'll do by best," she told her helplessly. Lady Kilraven made no answer, her emaciated face composed in a ghastly preview of her final sleep, and Carlotta left her.

"We *were* brief!" Miss Mims, knitting in the window of the sitting room, sprang to her feet, summoning once more the camaraderie of the first person plural. "We were thoughtful!" She hurried to open the door into the corridor. "Now do rest before dinner. We *are* looking a little tired!"

"Are we?" Dazedly Carlotta passed a hand across her brow. "Yes, I expect we are." Miss Mims's face froze: was she being mocked? And then, just for an instant, the bright brown eyes, pledged to welcome, showed their hate.

The hush which had settled on the castle was most noticeable before dinner. The staircase down which guests had come at this hour, the golden hall, the library where they had gathered cheerily for cocktails, were silent and empty.

Or nearly empty. A single woman huddled before the fire in a shapeless sweater.

Once more Carlotta came to a speechless halt. The woman, lank-haired, was pressed back in an easy chair as though cowering, her shoulders rounded, one foot tucked under her and one leg dangling, holding a drink on her knee, and the hearth fire unkindly underlighted two semicircular pouches topping her cheekbones. The topaz eyes told Carlotta this was Moira.

"It's cold in here," she announced flatly, the eyes resting on Carlotta in a steady, disinterested stare.

"Yes. Hello, Moira. Shall I do something about the fire?"

"No. You can't do anything about this fire. If you touch it at all it smokes. Only Hannan understands it. Leave it. You're back." The phrases came out between short pauses in which she seemed barely to breathe.

"Yes." To steady herself Carlotta moved away to the bar tray in the corner. A sense of calamity had suddenly come down over her like a hood, dislocating her from reality. Her knees wobbled. The altered appearance of an old woman was sad enough, but the change in Moira, un-

132

disguised, stated like a fact, was almost sinister. Carlotta hunched her own shoulders against a chill and splashed something into a glass. This afternoon she had stood aside and marveled at herself involved in the accelerating melodrama of Kilraven. Now for the first time fear, the well-named nameless fear, folded itself over her like bat wings, cutting her off from confidence and common sense, all but extinguishing her.

She made herself turn and cross to the sofa opposite Moira, still under her impassive stare, and forced herself to raise her eyes, averting their focus from the pouches blighting Moira's cheekbones like growths. She said as steadily as she was able, "Yes, I'm back. I've seen Lady Kilraven."

Moira twisted her lips, as if debating whether to comment, deciding evidently not to. Her stare fell to the drink in her hand balanced on her knee, the knee of the dangling leg, and she was silent. Carlotta realized she hadn't lifted the glass, hadn't moved her body a fraction of an inch except, shallowly and slowly, to breathe.

"I ran into Dermot in the lobby of the Shelbourne." She was determined to rouse Moira somehow. Her fear receded now under a mounting indignation, a recoil of the sensibilities Moira had produced in her before.

"Ah." The topaz eyes flicked a glance at Carlotta and fell to the glass again, and the brief syllable contained a volume of cynical amusement and indifference. "How was the dear lad?"

"Quite as usual. He was dining with cronies."

"Ah yes. His cronies. An earl without a farthing, a millionaire horse thief, a doctor who writes poetry, and a few other oddballs, as Sheilah would say. They gather round a table and roar at each other. Is Dermot in love with you?"

Color flared up in Carlotta's cheeks, and Moira was

watching her with a little twist of a smile, but she managed to answer lightly, "I doubt it."

"You doubt it. Well, he's likely to be. You're just the kind of scrupulous person he'd turn to now. Oh yes, I think he must be, to judge from your astonished face. Poor Dermot. He wouldn't stand a chance of getting you to bed, would he?" She uttered a staccato, mirthless, "Ha!" and continued in her husky drawl, "He's not a man to be taken lightly, you know. No wonder he's in such a fury."

Carlotta had to laugh; she had set out to disconcert Moira! The sound of her own laughter steadied her, but she didn't trust herself to speak, and now Moira moved at last, groaning a little as if she had rheumatism, putting both feet to the floor and leaning forward over the glass she still hadn't lifted to her lips.

She was ill, obviously; her talk was the impervious, impulsive kind uttered by a person drunk, distraught, or in pain, but she was not drunk, and whether she was distraught or really in pain Carlotta couldn't tell. The pouches under her eyes gleamed with the sheen of delicate skin abnormally swollen, her color was dull, and deeper and browner lines dragged from nose to mouth; but the symptom that seemed to Carlotta most pitiable was her untidy, not altogether clean, waif-like sweater.

"He wishes I were dead, you know," Moira stated, as if enthralled, her eyes wide to the firelight. "He hasn't said so, of course, and perhaps he doesn't even know it. But it's true, he's finally fed to the teeth with me."

"Wishing someone were dead and being fed to the teeth aren't the same."

"To me they're the same."

"Moira—"

"Oh, do shut up! You don't know anything about it and it has nothing to do with you. It's been a-building for

134

years. I'm fed to the teeth as well. Oh, fed, fed, to the teeth! Did he tell you he was in Dublin to deliver my horse, Finn McCool, to its new owner?" She pulled the corners of her mouth down in a hideous, brief, mock grimace like a tragic mask. "It's hardly worth mentioning." She turned her glassy stare on Carlotta. "You've come back. They sent for you, didn't they? Her ladyship and the inscrutable Dr. Fabret. Why do you let yourself be put upon? Are you all tender mush inside? If I were you I'd tell the lot of us to go to hell and take the first plane back to the States. Right now. Because if you don't," she added thoughtfully, "I think you're going to wish you had."

Carlotta closed her eyes and clung once more to her own identity. "I've been invited for a few days—that's four or five at the most, surely." Every sentence they uttered seemed to lead them further away from reality, further into the deep murky waters, the never-never land, of Kilraven's nebulous suffering. "I don't know if I'll be of any use or not, but if it's possible to help someone—"

"Help someone!" Moira pounced, her voice, suddenly raw and rasping, cutting through Carlotta's as if out of ambush. "My God, what we've endured for that man— for that thing that's left of a man, what we've denied ourselves to keep him up there like a decaying vegetable!" She leaned forward, bending almost double, still gripping her glass with both hands so that its rim pressed into her breast. "Have you any idea of the suffering he has caused, he and his mad, criminal, obsessed mother? Have you any idea what it's been like for Dermot, breaking his heart to keep this demesne together, for *him*, for a half-creature no one's even allowed to set eyes on? Selling my horse is merely one more sickening deed done for that creature in the name of service. It's he, Michael, who's come between Dermot and me, whose slow rot has poisoned us! And

135

now, before she dies, his doting mother is pulling every string, calling in every Jack and Jill, patching him up, propping him up, so that he may come out of hiding at last and outlive us all!"

She tipped forward onto her feet and staggered to the hearth where she thrust her glass on the shelf and stood clutching the carved edge of the mantel.

The violence of her paroxysm held Carlotta speechless. Gothic words—*rot, poison, mad*—seemed to vibrate in a ruby light before her eyes.

"Good evening, Moira." It was Edward, decompressing the turgid silence with his entrance, and reason settled on the room at last. Contemptuously Moira's eyes glanced at him and back to the firelight and she didn't answer. He bent over Carlotta. "How's your drink? How's yours, Moira?"

"Thank you," she said inconsequentially, from the distance into which she had withdrawn once more. "Tell them I shan't stay to dinner after all. Good night." And with a curious awkwardness, rheumatically, she left the room.

"Oh, Edward," groaned Carlotta, "I'm glad you're here."

He was at the tray in the corner. "It's stopped raining. We might go out for a breath of fresh air after dinner."

"Fresh air! Oh, yes, let's." What a rock of sanity he was. "Edward, what's happened to Moira? What's the matter with her?"

"Pills, I think."

"Pills?"

"Barbiturates, I would guess." He crossed the room and sat down beside her. "I gather, to call a spade a spade in your terms, she goes on binges now and then."

"That's dangerous, isn't it?"

"Of course."

She set her teeth together and hunched her shoulders. Beneath the melodrama, she realized, behind the secrecy, the evil looks and lurkings, there was indeed suffering, a real suffering, and she was only beginning to comprehend the magnitude of it. Her bystander role of innocence, she told herself, mustn't promote itself into insensibility. The revelations of the past few hours, however incomplete, had strangely reshaped the familiar outlines of things at Kilraven, loosened her preconceptions; even this once sociable room appeared different, as though she had come into it for the first time.

"Drink up," said Edward, firmly taking hold of her wrist for an instant. "It's nearly time for dinner. Miss Mims is staying with Lady Kilraven. Do you suppose Hannan will beat the gong just for us?"

But Hannan appeared noiselessly in the door, his young, pallid face as discreetly blank as he could make it; something in the set of his shoulders gave the impression that he had just disengaged himself from a pantry quarrel. Everything had changed at Kilraven, everyone was shaken, the once tightly reined household fearful of the loosening grip.

"Dinner is served, Madam," he said resolutely.

They walked all the way to the gates, accompanied by Seamus, the golden dog. The moon, nearly full again, made a pale blur behind the clouds, and a heavy wet stillness blanketed the night, broken only by an inquiring bark from a distant corner of the demesne and the remote, self-absorbed rumble of a transatlantic plane. The damp scented air cleared their heads and they walked with a grateful sense of liberation.

At Edward's prompting Carlotta described her childhood, her naturalist father and poetic Irish mother, a "liberal" New England background with its strong overtones of propriety; and on the return trip from the gates she persuaded Edward to tell her something of his own upbringing in Baltimore in an atmosphere of high intellect, both his parents being physicians, a childhood that sounded to Carlotta scholarly, single-minded, and lonely.

Unconsciously she stiffened and grew silent as the castle loomed over the lake once more, a vague mass against the pale clouds. Except for the light in Carlotta's room, the north tower was dark.

She was used by now to Edward's reading her thoughts. "It might ease your mind," he told her, "to know I've changed my room to the one next to yours."

She let out her breath, not realizing she had been holding it. "I'm glad. I was just thinking how I should miss Fran—knowing she was there."

"You'll call me if you want me."

"Of course."

At her door he kissed her lightly on the cheek and said good night.

She undressed and put on her robe and lay down on her bed. No Mozartian summons sounded; the night was perfectly silent. And after a long day of driving, of dread and dismay and numbing rain, her eyes closed in spite of herself.

It was still dark when she awoke. The lamp she had left on had been turned off. She lay perfectly still while her eyes adjusted to the darkness. In a few seconds she made out the gray square of her open window. There was no sound but the tiny tick of her traveling clock, no intake of breath, but she knew with the sudden cooling of her skin that she was not alone, that someone stood quite close to her. And a moment later she distinguished the shape, motionless and pale, beside her bed.

It never occurred to her to call out to Edward. Slowly,

as though weights or drugs burdened her, she dragged herself into a half-sitting position. "Michael?" she whispered; hopefully and fearfully, as she had done once before. "Michael?"

The pale blur retreated. In the next instant she heard the soft click of her door closing. She turned on her lamp. She was alone.

❦ 10

J.J. paced in the driveway beside his Bentley. He was
smoking a cigar and looking fresh as paint, his cheeks
rosy over a blue bow tie. The sun was shining and the
birds were singing. His sharp eyes scrutinized Carlotta
as she came down the steps to greet him and he said without preamble, "I stopped by to check on you. How are
you?"

"I'm fine, J.J. How nice of you. You *are* a welcome
sight. Are you all at Rossgharda now?"

"All but Tony, who had to stick at his drafting board in
Dublin. I don't know how Constance is going to paint
Sheilah without that boy around; the air has gone right
out of her." He pursed his lips and gazed across the park.
"What do *you* think, Carlotta? D'you think we're too hard
on her, making her go back to the States with us?"

"Yes," she said.

The sharp eyes swung around to her in surprise.
"Seventeen," he said severely. "Fresh out of school."

"She's got her father's mind, however undeveloped,
and her mother's backbone."

He puffed on his cigar, his eyes steady on her face, and
she was mindful of the hosts of men in the world of J.J.'s
complex business interests who must have had to hold
their ground under this stare. "In my book," he told her
at last, somewhat mystifyingly, "there are three useless

things to indulge in: worry, regret, and stubbornness. I appreciate your candor."

He took her arm and drew her down the drive. "Let's get out of earshot. I don't trust that snoopy little Englishwoman. Are you really all right? There's no funny business going on? You have only to say the word," the cool competent readiness to shepherd gleamed in his eyes, "and I'll move you out of here this minute."

It seemed a shame to deny him this rescue. "J.J., I really am all right."

Monstrous clouds, left over from the rainstorm, were piled in discard on the horizon, and the sky was intensely blue. What a pleasant pastime, she had been thinking, framing a mental long-shot of themselves on the drive, to chat with a caller in the morning sun! She must have dreamed—she must have—of the intruder in her room last night.

"Well, you've got friends an hour away, don't forget that." They returned to J.J.'s car. "I was delegated to invite you and Dr. Fabret to dinner tonight. No, don't say no. Just come." He was about to insert his neat little behind in the leather bucket seat when he paused and looked up at the battlements. "Too bad," he said. "This place will have to go someday, I suppose. Americans will buy it, make a hotel of it. Or better still, a private club." He checked himself, frowning reprovingly. "Give Lady Kilraven my respects. Tell her I'm at her service." He got into the car. "At seven," he advised Carlotta, and drove off purposefully.

Carlotta gave a sigh of momentary contentment. What could threaten with J. J. Malloy in the vicinity? A blackbird warbled a pensive statement somewhere under the spreading trees of the park. She felt the urge to paint again and turning, she lifted her eyes just in time to see

Miss Mims withdraw from the sitting-room window. She sighed again, resignedly.

The gravel crackled a second time and a dusty Volkswagen whirled into the drive and halted before the steps. A shaggy man in his fifties, shapeless and red-eyed, as though one more sleepless night would see him come unstuck altogether, emerged with a small black medicine bag.

"Burke," he said, with a real roll of the *r*, thrusting out his hand and doffing a weather-stained hat, a practiced series of motions involving the rapid shifting of his bag. "Charming morning, isn't it? On a day like this my thoughts turn to Lough Mask even if the salmon would be hiding from the sun." He was climbing the steps with Carlotta, propelling her along with him by means of his conversation alone. "You're American, of course. I have a sister in New York and a dozen distant cousins in Boston, as who has not? Have ye seen the Niagara Falls?" He performed an agile, automatic shuffle on the door mat. "But 'A man travels the world over in search of what he needs and returns home to find it.' D'ye read our own George Moore at all? Few people do any more. A whole new litter of young writers claim the Irish scene and I say God love them!" Now they were moving rapidly down the great hall. "When the day arrives that we deplore the new and yearn for the old we're past our prime, are we not? Today! That is the magic word! 'Today welllived makes every yesterday a dream of happiness and every tomorrow a vision of hope.' Good health to you." And he veered off abruptly into the corridor leading to Lady Kilraven's rooms.

Carlotta painted the old ruin and enjoyed a picnic lunch in the sun in the company of the tower's dedicated occupants, the nesting jackdaws, and in the afternoon she deliberately chose once more the view of the castle from across the lake, a site she knew could be seen from the north tower. Without raising her field glasses she felt certain she was under surveillance. The sketch turned out badly. She walked back to the castle.

Miss Mims was working at a desk in the sitting room. She got quickly to her feet. "Lady Kilraven is sleeping," she told Carlotta, not smiling. They regarded each other for a moment, and some kind of deliberation took place behind Miss Mims's bright brown eyes. She asked suddenly, "Won't you come in and sit down for a moment?"

"Thank you, but——"

"Please do."

It was both plea and demand. Was a peace offering to be made, or a declaration of war? Or was Miss Mims merely lonely?

As Carlotta hesitated Miss Mims sprang into action, summoning the old archness, throwing in everything that came to hand in the line of persuasion. "Here is a comfortable chair by the window. I opened it as it was so warm, almost like summer, don't you think? It won't be too cool for you, will it? How unnaturally quiet it is! I can't get used to it, not having the castle full of people, not having Lady Kilraven——" Her voice caught and she cleared her throat and went rapidly on. Carlotta found herself seated by the window. "Let me relieve you of your things. You've been sketching, haven't you? May I look? May I see what you've done? Charming! The ruin, of course. You've even put the jackdaws in. How clever you are. And the castle. The famous view. Yes, delightful."

She deposited the sketches carefully on the desk and sat down primly in a straight chair opposite Carlotta. She said, "He'll like them."

"I hope so," replied Carlotta, without an outward start, but inwardly leaping to astonished attention.

But perhaps Miss Mims was not cut out, after all, for this kind of cat and mouse play, or she was under too much strain. Without warning the shoe-button eyes, dark-ringed, filled with tears. Desperately they roved to the window, blinking frantically, and a harrowing flush rose from Miss Mims's neck to her scalp, mottling her brow.

And even though it meant saving her for further skirmishing, Carlotta threw out a lifeline. "How long," she asked quietly, "have you been at Kilraven?"

Miss Mims grasped at it. "Ten years." The lids blinked, the flush subsided. "Ten years next September." She had got control of herself; she studied her hands. "I came straight from the vicarage in Sussex. My father had been in failing health for a long time, and I had been secretary to the Countess of Byeford in Lovell Hall outside the village. I commuted daily on my bicycle. After my father's death I—felt I needed a change, and through connections I learned that Lady Kilraven was looking for someone."

Carlotta, giving rein to her imagination again, pictured Miss Mims, not a day younger, settling a rotund little vicar in a four-poster with his medicine, his hot-water bottle, a clerical volume or two (or an Agatha Christie mystery?), and peddling off in the rain, down a poplar-lined avenue to a damp gray Lovell Hall, where a horse-faced Countess of Byeford, strident and exacting, sat her down in a cheerless library. . . . And this dogged, even valiant little woman of the past was then irrevocably bound in Carlotta's mind with the present Miss Mims.

In spite of herself, without knowing it or perhaps without knowing why, Miss Mims went on confiding in her enemy. "Lady Kilraven had begun to take in paying guests. It was not easy for her. It meant a radical change in her life. But something had to be done to augment the

144

income of the demesne and she faced up to it squarely. It has taken its toll." She lifted her eyes and turned her head to the bedroom behind her. She hung on the brink of tears again. O'Connell had mentioned their long power struggle. It was a contest Lady Kilraven had obviously won by default, and perhaps this was why Miss Mims had to talk to Carlotta: only a trustworthy adversary could sustain her now.

"You were here then," Carlotta persisted unobtrusively, "at the time of Michael's accident?"

"No." And a faint veil of superiority dropped over Miss Mims's eyes; she was in the know and Carlotta was not. "I was here when he was brought home."

"From France?"

"From Switzerland. Lady Kilraven had exhausted every possibility for his recovery."

"Had she announced his death?"

"She didn't have to." Miss Mims was examining her hands again. "She—you might say, allowed the mistake to be made. It evolved. The French, I believe, were the first to report his death, and the Irish took it up, publishing his obituaries, and Lady Kilraven never corrected them. You find it hard to believe?" Her eyes leveled on Carlotta's. "It was the kindest thing she could have done for him."

Carlotta heard her own quick intake of breath. But she wouldn't argue the point. "Then how did he—how did she manage to—"

"He was registered everywhere as Thomas Fenn, which happen to be two of his rightful names. But there are hundreds of Thomas Fenns in this region, just as there are hundreds of Thomas Quinns in the Quinn region. He was flown to Shannon in a privately chartered plane. And in order not to attract attention, it was I," she closed her eyes solemnly, "whom Lady Kilraven chose to meet him that night and drive him home.

"And for years," Miss Mims continued, her voice dropping suddenly to a stifled whisper, saliva collecting in the corners of her mouth, "I was the only one he would allow near him. Not even his own mother. No! He never forgave her. It was I who took his meals to him, saw to his needs—his books, his records. It wasn't for nothing that I had taken care of my father so long. Michael trusted me. I was the only one he trusted. It was I who mothered him—!" She checked herself in mid-gasp, her billowed shirtwaist rising and falling, her eyes blazing on Carlotta. She veiled them again. She concluded darkly, austerely, in Charlotte Brontë prose: "Until you appeared, unbidden, on our doorstep."

"Dr. Fabret had already appeared, bidden, before me. Miss Mims, surely you can't resent Michael's showing improvement for someone else?"

"I resent his showing improvement at all!" Miss Mims was on her feet, her hands clenched at her sides, and Carlotta sat thunderstruck. "This is what I wanted to say to you. He is better off where he is, removed from life. Life has nothing to offer him but humiliation and misery. He would be better off dead!"

"How can you say that?" Carlotta, striving to keep her voice down, was also on her feet. "Even Lady Kilraven doesn't believe he should be shut away any more."

"She changed her mind only because she realized he was going to outlive her."

"But of course he will! Why, why have you all conspired so, why—"

"Why?" whispered Miss Mims, suddenly quieting ominously. She smiled, she wore a look of perfect, almost beatified, triumph. "Why?" In the hush the birds seemed to burst into song again. "Perhaps I should tell you. Perhaps someone really should tell you, once and for all—break our pledge at last, and put an end to your foolish blundering. You really want to know why?"

Carlotta nodded, holding her breath, spellbound by Miss Mims's gladiator smile; even the birds hushed.

And then from the next room came the faint tinkle of a bell. Miss Mims's smile faded, her jaw dropped, her teeth showed, her hand gripped the back of the little chair. They confronted each other for a moment longer. A hiss of breath came from between the bared teeth. A kind of despair loosened the skin of the round face. "That was Lady Kilraven," she whispered, defeated once more. It was almost as if a voice from the dead had silenced her. "You must excuse me now." And she turned and vanished into the bedroom.

Carlotta came down the great staircase coolly dressed in white for dinner at Rossgharda. At the foot of the stairs she found herself face to face with Dermot Fenn. He had evidently just returned; he wore the same costume he had worn in Dublin and was about to turn the corner into Lady Kilraven's corridor. Her very dread of encountering him had kept her from preparing herself for the possibility, and obviously he wasn't prepared to find her here. A look of amazed dismay blanked his face and brought him to a standstill.

A half-apology rose to her tongue, but the violence of his farewell at the Shelbourne came over her again in a hot gust. "Lady Kilraven sent for me," she told him hopelessly.

And what was going on behind the piercing, noncommittal, Fenn-blue eyes? He looked at her a moment longer and then uttered a sound of acknowledgment, nodding shortly. He moved on, his light, deceptively diffident step fading away down the corridor.

Her jaw clenched, her brow troubled, she went out to meet Edward in the drive. If he noticed her discomposure he kept discreetly silent, and it wasn't until they were on their way back to Kilraven, several hours later, that he brought the matter up.

It had been a relaxed and refreshing evening. For a little while Carlotta was able to throw off her burden of anxiety, a burden she was aware of only then, when she was free of it. There was a great deal of love in the reunion at Rossgharda. This was not alone the heightened fraternity of compatriots in a foreign land, for it was Constance Temple's home and Constance Temple's concern and warmth that drew them together. They felt, all of them, including Edward Fabret, that it was a time and place and mood they might never create together again, a moment of ease and safety, a respite.

After dinner, before the light failed, they strolled through the burgeoning garden to the studio and viewed a half-formed vision of Sheilah, taking shape out of floating pale-greens and violets. Then Sheilah herself, all but lifeless without Tony, bade them "love-love" and went off to bed, and Conor O'Connell asked Constance to sing. She sang only one song and unaccustomed tears stood in Fran's eyes and J.J. patted her hand. Then Constance got them all to singing, and at the end of the evening they found themselves, dumbfounded, listening to Edward Fabret delivering "Kathleen Mavourneen" in a clear, resolute tenor.

O'Connell muttered in Carlotta's ear, "At last I like the man."

"We always had music at home," Edward told her on the ride home. "Traditional outlet for medical eggheads. I play the violin a little, as a matter of fact."

She turned to him, smiling, picturing him with the

148

serious, motherly expression fiddlers wear, the instrument tucked under his chin on a little diaper. "Tell me more," she exclaimed softly, in awe of his hidden facets.

"I'm a fool for bagpipes, harpsichords, and Gilbert and Sullivan."

"Edward, what else! Chess? Tennis?"

"I used to be rather good at figure skating."

"Of course!"

"And I play a mean game of cribbage."

"Ah! Any man who plays cribbage can't be all bad."

He grinned. "You're feeling more like yourself, aren't you?"

"Yes, I suppose I am." But the realization brought from her a quick, haunted sigh. They passed through a sleeping town of gray stone, its steep, parochial roofs shining in the moonlight.

"Dermot Fenn," said Edward suddenly, his voice, perhaps in an effort to sound casual, rising to an unusual pitch, "was going in just as you came out this evening. Did you see him?"

She turned to him curiously. "I saw him." And her heart, lulled by affection, dulled by dread, came to with a start.

"Attractive fellow, isn't he?"

She began to smile. "Yes, in a way."

"In what way, do you think?"

She laughed. "How ingenuous you are, Dr. Fabret."

"No, seriously," he protested, and then a little puff of a laugh came from him also. "Well, damn it, perhaps I am." He frowned. "Interesting. You don't suppose I could be a little jealous, do you?"

"You're the doctor."

"I mean, I really thought I was interested in your attraction to the man."

"I think you really are."

"You *are* attracted to him, then!"

"You were the one who said he was attractive."

He sat back grimly. A vague huffiness filled the air. "What I was getting at," he began carefully again, "was that you seemed upset when you came out."

"Perhaps I was, a little. It wasn't important."

"Anything that upsets you is important." Her eyes were on the verge of misting again when he added, "Anything that upsets anyone, even a little. Especially a little."

She made no comment. "Edward," she asked gently after a time, "have you never been jealous before?"

"I *must* have been!" he exclaimed, scowling.

She smiled. "Edward, you can get quite stuffily angry, you play the violin, you are capable of jealousy. You grow more and more likable!"

"That's damn faint praise if I ever heard it."

"I mean, you don't have to be so objective."

"I'm *not* so objective!"

"I'm glad."

He brooded and they entered the gates of Kilraven Castle.

"Oh, God, Edward, I'm afraid. I'm afraid."

He stopped the car at once and took both her hands. "Then go, tomorrow. Tonight, if you like."

"No, not if Michael wants to see me."

"I'm certain he does want to. In fact, I think now he wants you to know him as he really is. It isn't easy for him."

She drew in a long breath. "Miss Mims almost told me this afternoon. I don't know *what* she was going to tell me, but I'm sure it was whatever I can't understand about him, about all of you. Edward," she pleaded, "won't you tell me?"

"Don't you see, he must tell you himself! It will be a

major step in his recovery if he can tell you. It will be a real victory. Perhaps tonight he'll be able to."

She let her breath out in a long shudder. She sat for a moment with her hands tightly clasped between his. "Edward, I have to tell you this even though it may sound hysterical. I don't even know why I feel this way. A number of frightening things have been said about Michael since yesterday but it really isn't anything anyone has said. It's just that I feel—I sense something terribly ominous. I feel—as if—as if *somebody is going to die*. I'm not awfully worried about myself. But I am worried about Michael. Edward, I feel he is in danger!"

He was silent a moment. He released her hands and put the car in gear. His breath whistled between his teeth. "I hope you're wrong."

There were cars in the driveway, too many cars. The dusty Volkswagen was at the door. Dr. Burke, just coming out with his black bag, met them at the top of the steps, his face, which this morning had seemed so disheveled, strangely put to rights. Lady Kilraven, he told them, was dead.

11

The castle, ablaze with light, was awake all night with muffled comings and goings, and at daybreak a line of carts and automobiles, mourners on donkeys, on horseback, and on foot, began to crawl up the drive. "The rank and file," said the red-cheeked Mary, case-hardened—indeed wakes were more familiar to her than weddings— "the rank and file will give way to the gentry, and last of all the lords and ladies will be arriving."

The casket lay in state in the darkened drawing room. The mourners whispered Catholic prayers over it even though Lady Kilraven was professedly Protestant and privately agnostic, and then they filed into the dining room where the Waterford decanters were set out under Hannan's mistrustful eye.

Mary had brought a sandwich and a cup of tea to Carlotta in the library, where she had volunteered to answer the telephone, incessantly ringing, and to notify distant relatives. Everything else fell upon Miss Mims. Dermot, nominally in charge, had little knowledge of the mechanics of the household, and Moira, presumably holed up again, never appeared at all.

"This was thoughtful of you," said Carlotta gratefully, easing her shoulder blades.

"To tell the truth, madam, 'twas Miss Mims sent me.

Not that I wouldn't have brought it meself had I known ye'd missed yer lunch."

Miss Mims, ever-mindful of her foes! Serving those she resented, resenting those she served, and helpless to reverse her role. . . . Did she harbor secretly this same hate for Michael?

Mary, gazing out the window, her hands clasped palms down over her apron, asked the unanswerable question: "Will there never be gladness in this house?"

The telephone rang and Mary went away. Fran and J.J. knocked and stopped to offer assistance, urging her again to come to Rossgharda. Later Edward came in and perched for a moment on the corner of the desk.

He had taken lately to giving her a visual checkup for signs of strain, his glance traveling quickly over her face and hands. "There's a marvelous collection of people out there," he told her. "It's like a procession of Abbey players."

"It sounds like monks muttering in the cloister of a monastery. One thing is missing, Edward. Have you noticed?"

"What's that?"

"Tears. I've seen respect and regret and even sadness, but I haven't seen one person, not even Miss Mims, shed a tear."

He said, looking down at his flexed knee, "I have."

Her own throat tightened suddenly. "Michael?"

"Michael."

"He's forgiven her then!"

"I don't think so. It's more like a release from nonforgiveness. He weeps easily."

"Perhaps they all feel this release, here in the castle. She dominated their lives."

"Some of them put it another way: *he* dominated their lives."

"Yes. That's what I was trying to tell you last night. Edward, have you any idea of the bitterness that's built up against him?"

"Of course."

"He didn't send for me again. That's the second night."

"He couldn't, with the place in such an upheaval. There wasn't a moment of quiet—"

The telephone interrupted, and Carlotta was entangled in a faulty trunk call from a Miss Philomena Fenn in London. When she hung up Edward had left.

Lastly Miss Mims entered, saying, "Everything is going quite smoothly. I can take the calls now. You had better rest."

"Isn't it you, Miss Mims, who needs rest? You were up all night."

Miss Mims gave her a level stare. "You must not concern yourself with my welfare."

"Well, I shall," said Carlotta equably, "whether you like it or not." She couldn't have told Miss Mims this a month ago. In fact were it not for the something adamantly eerie in Miss Mims's make-up, the unpredictable threat of the spinster, the indiscriminate vengefulness of the dutiful, she might almost have liked her, for now Miss Mims was not so much of a mystery, and Carlotta had seen her tears of frustration, and almost as vividly seen her peddling her bicycle in the rain.

Miss Mims blinked her eyes rapidly. "You must suit yourself then," she mumbled, at a loss. She collected herself, stretched up her chin. "I want you to know, Mrs. Fleet, that I shall continue to regard you as Lady Kilraven's guest as long as you stay here."

"That's all right," replied Carlotta, rising, meanly not volunteering the information she knew Miss Mims was dying for." "Here are the calls I've received, and here are the ones I've put through. The Reverend Pennel wants you to call him back, and Colonel Fenn says he will arrive in time for dinner . . ."

The line in the hall had fallen off, but a strong odor of spirits and cigar smoke and a mutter of male voices came from the dining room, as though a business conference were being held there. Carlotta opened the drawing-room door.

She stepped into a dream-cave, the stillest of places in a living world. The drawn curtains produced a lavender dusk, and sprays of flowers made stalactites and stalagmites. The massed scents formed a breathlessnes, a tomb of heavenly stillness. In the center, under a blanket of white roses, slept the stillest person of the stillest place. The twilight, the hush, the immobile blossoms, attended her, guarded her, concentrated purposefully on her repose. It was like stepping into the core of sleep. What was death like? This, the cave pronounced, was what it was like, cool and exotic.

The casket was mercifully closed. Carlotta didn't want to have to look upon that grotesquely childlike body again, and, at the opposite end of time, the conclusive skull. She stood for a moment beside the casket, her hands folded.

From an incorrigibly complicated woman Augusta Fenn had become incorrigibly simple. There was no need any longer to decide if she had been courageous or criminal or both. She had been human; she was no longer. "I'm sorry," Carlotta told her silently, "I'm sorry." Where Augusta had failed she had hoped Carlotta might succeed, impossibly taking upon herself the attributes of Constance Temple, Miss Mims, and Dr. Fabret, all in one. It was too late; if Carlotta succeeded, Augusta Fenn would never know about it. The removal of Augusta's terrible will had left a vacuum. Her will and her gratification were

155

needed. Without them, Carlotta was already apologizing for her failure.

She said for the soul of Augusta Fenn one of her very personal, highly informal prayers, certain of a listener, and turned about, and sucked in her breath in a gasp that was almost a scream. Behind her, a figure sat motionless among the floral sprays.

It came to life, it rose slowly, became Dermot Fenn, cap in hand. (Had he been mourning the old soldier?) "Are you going back to the library now?"

"No, Miss Mims has taken over." She swallowed, trying to get her breath, her pulse thudding. "I was going out for a little walk. But if there's something I can do—"

"I'd like a word with you, if you'll do me the favor. You'll take the path into the park? I'll catch you up."

The day had clouded over. It was a white, quiet, afternoon, the quietness seeming to deepen from moment to moment and the humidity bringing up odors of vegetation. Carlotta moved into a sultry gloom of foliage. Nothing was dead here, everything was subtly alive, even the organic minutiae of rot, of compost underfoot, of moss and ferns. A pond was a biologist's paradise of green scum. Everything was silently living, breathing, and it was as if the neglected park would endure forever, reverting to the primeval. This was real, Carlotta told herself, and the cave of permanent sleep was abstract, a moment of the imagination; this was life, secretly breathing the centuries away, and Augusta Fenn had merely cast a fleeting shadow.

The humidity collected under the sleeves of her jacket and she took it off and tied the sleeves around her waist. She didn't hear the soft thud of horse's hooves until they were close behind her. Dermot dismounted lightly and walked beside her. He said, "One for sorrow." When she

156

looked at him for explanation he pointed out a magpie, flashing black and white as it rose from a distant field. "It's a rhyme we use when we see magpies." He recited it for her.

> *"One for sorrow,*
> *Two for joy,*
> *Three for a girl,*
> *Four for a boy.*
> *Five for England,*
> *Six for France,*
> *Seven for a wedding,*
> *Eight for a dance. . . ."*

They had entered the beech woods, stately and still, and they walked in silence until they reached the clearing around the temple. Even Dermot's nervous beast was subdued and fell to cropping grass. In silent agreement they climbed the rise and sat down on the temple's shallow steps.

"Well, now," he said at last in a leaden voice, after gazing a long moment into the dark leaves of the rhododendrons below, "I've followed you out here, I'd better say what I've got to say."

She had been facing straight ahead also, waiting half-fearfully, and she turned to him now, wondering. He was not ill at ease or putting on his rustic manner, but he seemed oppressed. Perhaps he had loved Augusta Fenn. Or perhaps the sultriness, the white light now settling, darkening slightly, turning green at the edges, and the greenish scents of decay, weighed on him.

"The trouble is," he continued with a kind of methodical pessimism, "when I get near to you I want only to take you in my arms."

She drew in her breath slowly.

"Ah, no, don't worry. It was to make amends that I asked to see you. That and one other thing. I may never have the chance again to talk to you alone." He was still addressing the foliage at the bottom of the slope. "I won't apologize, mind you, I can't apologize, it's not in my nature to be false to myself." She suppressed a smile. His elbows rested across his spread knees and between them he tortured a willow switch that served for a crop, doubling it and unbending it. "Why should I apologize for kissing you or giving way to anger at your repulse? It's not a disgrace to you or to me to show my feelings, and I can't regret having them!" He had almost worked himself up to anger again, and she, too, was already controlling anger.

"Not even for Moira's sake?"

"For God's sake don't interrupt," he shouted, "or I'll never be able to—no, not even for Moira's sake! I ask you not to bring Moira into it. What I haven't a right to do is to go into what there is between Moira and me, what there ever was. Besides, she's not well now and can't speak for herself." He glowered at the shrubbery. His mare had ceased to crop and stood staring attentively into space as if engrossed in some lovely horse-fantasy, one hind ankle daintily crooked.

"I'm not a man of words, Carleen, like your Dr. Fabret, and I'm not in the habit of explaining myself, even to myself, but I live by my own standards and one of them is to be true to my own feelings. It's just as dishonorable to me to deny an honest feeling as it is to forge a name. But it's contrary as well to hurt a woman deliberately, a blameless woman, just for the sake of easing myself, and I can't forget the look in your face when you left me there in Dublin and I can't let that be the look I'll remember of you. What I want to say to you is that with all my heart I regret having caused you pain." His hands were still, clutching the willow switch, his calves drawn close in to his thighs; he seemed to hold his breath.

"Please forget the look," she told him, her throat and eyes smarting. "The pain is gone."

He turned to look at her briefly. "It's all right, then?"

"I wish I could deal as honestly with my own feelings."

"A woman's feelings are more subtle," he informed her, "and that's the difficulty."

"They allow themselves far more feelings."

"It must be terrible," he commiserated.

"It's complicating."

He was twisting the willow switch again, not looking at her. "One honest feeling," he told her slowly, "is complicating enough for me."

Her breath came shallowly then, her own heart expanding as if to receive his affliction. The hush of the humid afternoon had deepened, the sky was greener, the shadows blurred and darkening.

"Who will claim you, I wonder?" he asked in a low voice. "You'll not go unasked for, you're meant to be loved, and you've the need of someone to look after you. I shouldn't begrudge him, either, since I wouldn't wish you anything but happiness."

She held still, knowing there was nothing she could say that wouldn't complicate matters the more.

"At least," he continued, "I have another meeting with you to be thankful for. You keep coming back just when I think I'll never see you again. You nearly bowled me over in the hall yesterday. At least I haven't got to carry with me that look of disbelief, as if I'd struck you."

He turned slowly, his eyes lifted heavily to her face, his hand lifted and smoothed her hair, dropped to her shoulder and drew downward over her arm, came to rest over her hand. He smiled a little without humor. "Your eyes brim with tears," he murmured. "For me! For me,

159

I tell myself! You tremble on the brink, don't you? You could love me, couldn't you? You could love me now. I could kiss your sweet lips, kiss your tears, and take you over there to the shadows and fill you with love to over-flowing. I could make you forsake your conscience now, couldn't I, perhaps even because you pity me, I could ask you if this is so and you would answer yes."

"Yes," she cried softly, raising his hand to her cheek. "Yes, I would. Ask me."

"But how could I let you go then, and how could I make you stay? You would belong to me, and it would be like tearing apart my own flesh. For I am going to ask you to go."

She moaned, clinging to his hand, and in the distance the first mutter of thunder sounded.

"It came to me as you stood beside that coffin, alone in a strange house, like a prisoner. You don't belong here, we've no right to keep you. Things are changed now, there's no head of the household, no responsible head. There's no telling what may come about in the next few days. It's an unhealthy atmosphere for you; I don't like it. It may not be safe. I ask you to go." He uttered a short bark of a laugh. "That's a bit of irony, isn't it, that I should ask you to leave! Ah, God, my dear love, Carleen, Carleen, I do ask you to leave. For your own sake I want you to leave."

Her skin had cooled, the terrible premonition had come alive again as if stalking the decaying park she gazed on, as if muttering with the thunder. Augusta Fenn was dead, Carlotta owed her nothing now. Perhaps Michael *was* better off a recluse. It wasn't really her affair. Even Edward had said there were forces set against her. . . . "I'll go," she told him. "I'll go in the morning."

"Tonight," he insisted. "Now."

"Let me stay one more night!"

160

A long breath, a sigh, escaped him. "Ah, well, then." He turned away. "It's settled." He smote the earth between his knees with his whip, and rose, and drew her up. "So I'll say goodbye to you now, and wish you well, always." He held her with his cheek against hers, his hands soothing her back. "I haven't asked what your feelings about me are—I can't—I'm afraid to know." He breathed his short laugh again. "To think that I refused you when I could have had you. It must be that I love you, Carleen, it must, remember that." And without kissing her he suddenly pulled away from her, went quickly down the slope, untethered the mare and without looking back, his face reddened and harrowed, cantered away.

The storm broke during dinner. Colonel Donal Fenn, brother of Augusta and first of the clan to arrive, a white-mustached, stone-deaf old man with the familial heavy lids and remote blue eyes, sat through the electrical pandemonium in stately oblivion. Miss Mims, however, seemed charged by it; her eyes were dark-ringed, and after each thunder clap she surveyed the others with a thin, exultant smile, nostrils distended, as if she had commanded the fireworks herself. It was difficult to make conversation. Respect for the dead would have kept it subdued in any case, but the crashing overhead and the unceasing reverberations, the flickering light, interrupted them, commanded their attention, drowned them out. At one point rain lashed against the windows behind the drawn curtains as though someone were playing a garden hose over them. Edward, unusually thoughtful to begin with, gave up trying to talk and meditated, and Carlotta and Miss Mims carried the ball in an irrelevant, spasmodic fashion. Somewhere upstairs a door slammed and hurrying feet sounded in the hall. From the kitchen regions came a rising wail, perhaps keening, which ended chillingly before it reached its top note, stifled undoubtedly by the harassed Hannan. Seamus, the golden retriever, quaking and panting, invaded forbidden territory and came to press himself against the legs under the table. They were finishing dessert when a brain-jarring explosion, preceded by a pop like a blown fuse and a white light, sounded directly overhead, and the electric wall sconces went out. Miss Mims gave a little scream and even the old gentleman looked up enquiringly, as if wondering if a servant had dropped a plate. The smoking candle flames inclined this way and that, and Dermot Fenn in a dripping raincoat, his face streaked and blazing, stood in the doorway.

They stared at him as if his materializing out of this tumult were only part of the general phenomena, and the thunder cannonaded away to the horizon, grumbling insatiably. "Was she here?" Dermot demanded, his voice strangely hoarse, almost strangled, his feet poised apart, his crop gripped like a weapon in his fist. "Have you seen her? Have you seen Moira?"

No one could answer for a moment. The thunder crashed again. In the wavering light the blue eyes of a dozen Fenns looked down on them with Dermot—all, it seemed in the candlelight, with the same potential wildness; all except Michael over the fireplace, pale, introverted, anomalous. An old thought must have recurred to everyone seated there : Dermot Fenn should have been the master of Kilraven. "Have ye seen her at all?"

No one had seen her. "You don't think she's out in *this*—" began Miss Mims shrilly, and suddenly was still.

"She's out in it all right," he told them, his head quivering with a slight tremor. "She hasn't been here?"

The old Colonel turned to glare at Carlotta. "Is something amiss?" And the light of ancient campaigns awoke in his eyes.

162

Edward had been placing his rumpled napkin on the table when Dermot appeared and his hand still hovered on it. "What's happened?" he asked quietly, and everyone waited, appalled. It was then that Carlotta noticed what Miss Mims must have spied from the first: there was blood on the hem of Dermot's raincoat.

Rage, contempt, and the faintest, unwitting hint of admiration flashed from his eyes. "What's happened? She's shot my horse, that's what happened, and be damned to her. I'm going to find her. Keep her here if she comes." And he was gone.

Sickened, they rose silently, and slowly moved into the hall. Hannan had produced candlesticks for each of them. The hall was a faintly glowing cavern. The old Colonel's lids drooped almost shut. "Nothing's afoot? You'll not be needing me?" Gaily they signaled him that all was well. He took up his candle, bade them good night with an urgent nod, and trudged off to bed.

Miss Mims began to laugh softly. Edward moved to her. "You need rest," he told her firmly, gripping her arm. "Please go to bed now."

"Well, really!" flared Miss Mims, snatching her arm away, for even though she respected him, he was another archenemy. But she had been obeying orders all her life, and she subsided. "If you really think so, Doctor," she mewed coyly, and then she sighed, on the verge of tears. "Very well. I am tired." She rolled her eyes at Carlotta, baring her teeth in a dreadful smile. "And anyway three's a crowd!" Her eyes steadied for an instant. "How well will *you* sleep, Mrs. Fleet, with Lady Kilraven's remains in the drawing room, a thunderstorm overhead, and a madwoman loose on the grounds?" And she began to laugh quite obscenely.

"Now, then," said Edward, and led her away.

Carlotta waited alone in the shadowy hall, the dog

163

cowering at her feet. The storm was passing, there were longer pauses between lightning and thunder. She was so saturated with the sense of disaster that it no longer surprised her, scarcely even moved her. She stood perfectly still, her head bowed.

Edward emerged again out of the gloom. "What she really needs," he said, "is a hypo. And now you." He brought his candle closer. "I almost wish you were hysterical, too. This quietness is much more disturbing to me."

"Edward, I have to tell you something. Dermot has asked me to leave. It was practically an order."

"Well, thank God."

"You're not disappointed? I did insist on staying one more night."

"I wish you hadn't. I wish I'd given the order myself. Life here has changed since yesterday. Everyone is suddenly free to act out his resentments." He linked arms with her and drew her toward the stairs. "I want you to lock yourself in and stay there until morning. I'm going to help find Moira."

"I'm glad. I don't like the look of Dermot with that crop in his hand."

"Exactly. Come on, I want to see you to your room."

It was midnight when she opened her door. The hall was in semidarkness; the sky was clearing and moonlight appeared at the windows. Far away thunder still muttered. Edward's room was empty, its door ajar. A draft caught up the skirts of Carlotta's robe and rushed past her face. Somewhere around the turn of the corridor a clock ticked watchfully. She stood still for a moment with the draft fanning her, waiting for the pulsing sighs in her lungs to quiet.

She gathered up her skirts and without a sound went

up the stairs. At the last moment, with her knuckles an inch from the door, something asked her to reconsider, to turn back.

But through the door the stringed instruments were making their poignant offer, of unearthly beauty in return for earthly peace, the young composer's own improvident terms. Asking was so much more painful than granting, Carlotta thought, more yielding of heart than ever before, and this was an appeal she would never hear again, or answer.

She knocked softly.

The music ceased, the door opened, the cool and quivering hand drew her inside.

Moonlight, silver-pale, opened flowerlike at the window and then faded. Michael stood beside her, a gray shape, waiting for her to speak.

"I thought you weren't going to send for me again," she told him. He didn't answer. "I came back to Kilraven to see you."

"You went away," he said flatly.

"Yes. I had to go. I shall have to go again."

"My mother is dead. Everything will change now."

"I hope so."

"Why do you hope so?"

"You are needed, Michael. There's no reason for you to stay here any more."

"Isn't there?"

She heard the trace of a lisp again, and the note of premature defeat, of dread. How was it she could pity a tortured being so deeply and not love him? But it was as if there were no receptacle in him for another's love. Perhaps this accounted for his perversity, the disjointedness of his responses, peevish childishness alternating with reason and dignity, an effeminate lisp and masculine pride, a careless approximation of madness and his stand

165

for sanity: the warmth of love did not integrate him. At the very heart of him, the very core, there was a chilling absence, and where love ought to be there was none—even for himself.

She said, "It was your mother who kept you here."

"There was no other place for me," he answered without emotion. "It suited me, as well."

"It was a mistake, and she admitted it. She told me so before she died. She had already found Dr. Fabret to try to undo it, she encouraged me to help. Michael, it was her last wish, that you should leave this tower!" They were still standing in the darkness close to the door. She found his hand. "Michael, will you come down with me now, right now?"

"No! Wait!" He was seized with a fit of trembling. "There's something—" His voice shook in unison with his hand. Then he seemed to control himself, inhaling and exhaling a deep sighing breath. "There's something you'll have to know."

A spasm of pure terror curled its way over her from head to foot. She, too, took a deep breath. "Yes, Michael. Tell me."

He stood perfectly still, he was silent.

"Well, Michael?"

"I can't," he moaned. "I can't."

"You can," she insisted, not knowing what lay in store for them, her pulse almost stifling her. "You can."

"Someone is listening," he pleaded.

"No one is listening!" She threw open the door behind her. The draft swept past her ankles and knees again. There was absolute silence. And yet there was a listening quality in this hush, as if the castle itself in its omniscient way held its breath. Softly she closed the door. "There's no one there."

166

"Please, not yet, not just yet! Come and sit down, please sit down for a moment."

Touched by his entreaty, she let him guide her to a chair and he sat down somewhere near her as they had done before. His voice came in a whisper at last. "They all wish I had died."

"They wish you would either live or die."

"I don't believe they will let me live. Oftentimes I wish they would not. I should have died. I killed my wife."

"You didn't want to kill her!"

"Not consciously. Oh, yes, Dr. Fabret has uncovered this guilt, he has been helpful. It was partly because of this guilt that I was quite willing to shut myself away. You see, I belonged here at Kilraven, I had always wanted to come back, to come home, and I could not." He said matter-of-factly, "I married a whore."

For one insane moment she wanted to laugh. She clenched her teeth, and said at length, "That doesn't surprise me."

"Nor did it surprise Dr. Fabret. My wife was the antithesis of my mother, she had to be. But the fact remains I should have died with her."

"Only one thing remains, Michael: for you to forgive your mother."

"Is that true? Yes. Perhaps that is what Dr. Fabret wants, too. The one forgiveness I cannot give. All in this household I can forgive, except the one beyond forgiveness!" He had begun to cough strangely between phrases, as though weeping without tears, and yet in spite of these pauses a torrent of words poured from him. "All of the living who hate me or fear me! Dermot, my cousin, sweating his life out for a home he loves with his blood but that doesn't belong to him, and his venomous wife, and Miss Mims, with her jealous devotion—even the servants, even Constance Temple from whom my mother tried to force

167

love and who fears me! All of these people wish I had died and I can forgive them! This is what is left for me to live on with, this is what my mother bequeathed me, and she is the one you ask me to forgive!"

Carlotta was on her feet. "Michael, go down with me now. Let me take you to her. You won't have to look at her, but you will feel differently about her. She is removed from you. She is gone and you are alive. She's— she's almost one with the flowers. I know, I was there today. What I saw, or felt—erased everything I held against her. Go down with me!"

But he asked, "Why are you doing this for me?" He added tremulously, "Why do I have faith in you?"

"Because I'm not your mother. Because I'm not—her antithesis either. She herself sensed this."

There was a silence intense with some kind of resolution. Then "Come," he said at last, almost calmly, and an instant later his damp hand clasped her wrist again. "Come with me to the window."

They crossed a carpet. The moon was behind clouds. He drew her to the open window and the wet scents of the ground below, and waited. She waited, also, longing to clear her throat, choking on her own terror. She could hear his breath come and go between his teeth, as if with terrible intent. Outside, a silver-edged cloud raced swiftly toward the east; in another moment the moon would sail free. Oh God, she prayed, don't let me, don't let me—

The prayer was never finished. Cloud and moon separated, he stood with his back to the flooding light. She could see the record player and the mute disc. "They can patch up the side of a skull and a cheek and a chin," his voice whispered quickly, close to her, like the hasty voice that runs beside one in a nightmare, "they can even make something that resembles a nose, but an ear can't be reconstructed and an eye can't be replaced—"

168

"Michael, look at me!" she cried, for she had already guessed.

He moved from the window, turned with his back to the room, and the light fell full on his face, or all that was left of it.

"Now you understand, don't you?" he screamed between his teeth. "You see why I must stay here or die. No one could ever bear to look at me!"

But astonishingly, all terror had left her, and she found herself in a calm beyond herself. Something seemed to have given way in her, and she said quietly, "I can bear to. Until now, Michael, I could only pity you. But you have done this for me, and I can love you."

He bowed his head, leaned his mutilated brow against the window frame, his hands gripping the sill. A sound came from him like an ultimate relinquishment, and he clung there for an instant. When he lifted his head he tilted it back to the shower of light as if surrendering his hideousness.

And he turned at last and said, "Let us go down."

He took her hand, trembling once more, and for the first time without disguise he left the tower.

They found their way easily by the moonlit windows, and in any case Michael knew his way in the dark. The curious draft still rushed through the halls, the clock ticked. There was no other sound, but again Carlotta was conscious of a pervasive listening, a hush perhaps of waiting, as Michael Fenn, Lord Kilraven, made his journey from imprisonment into liberty.

He hesitated at the top of the great staircase; he came to a full stop, clinging to her hand. "Don't be afraid!" she cried softly, and always afterward, shutting her eyes in mute horror, she would remember how she urged him on.

A little smile found its way into the half-face. He straightened and perhaps this was the most heart-rending moment of all. "I'm not afraid," he said. He let go of her hand and offered her his arm as if they were about to descend to a fanfare. They went down the stairs.

The front doors had been left open or had blown open and the wind of the clearing storm swept silently up the golden hall to meet them. Far away a hound gave tongue to the moon briefly and then was still. The shapes of furniture crouched in the shadows and it was as if the darkness breathed, softly, in and out. A floorboard snapped.

Carlotta, intent only on Michael's freeing himself once and for all, could read no threat in these attendant shapes and sounds, was entirely innocent of any sense of danger, and perhaps in the long run this was as well.

He forgave his mother. It may have been that he had already made way for forgiveness in the tower he had left behind him, when he forgave himself. He stood over the embowered casket for a long moment, and the moonlight glimmered behind the drawn curtains. And finally he took up one of the white roses and brought it to his tortured lips and whispered, "Rest in peace," and those were his last words. He, too, had found peace.

The moonlight began to fade again, sucking away with it whatever light illuminated the room and the hall, and Carlotta, behind Michael and to one side of the door, remembered afterwards wondering if it were some extraordinary recurrence of the storm—the ensuing flash of light and the ear-splitting explosion. And then the night came to life in an inexplicable confusion, of footsteps running in the hall, a scream (Miss Mims, everlurking?), a car starting up and roaring away, boots plunging up the front steps and into the room, and Edward calling her name. She herself was kneeling beside Michael and holding him, saying to him again, over and over, as

170

if she knew this was to be his longest journey, "Don't be afraid, don't be afraid . . ."

She had no idea what had happened, except that Michael had fallen and his blood wetly warmed her hands.

Edward was holding a glass to her lips. She was in the library, wrapped in someone's pungent overcoat. The electricity had come on again and the room was brightly lighted. She had not lost consciousness exactly, but for a little while she seemed to have lost cognizance. Miss Mims was seated oddly at the desk on the other side of the room in an attitude of prayer, her head bowed on her clasped hands. Feet trampled in the hall beyond the closed door and peremptory voices sounded.

Over the glass she was searching Edward's eyes and he was searching hers, as if they hoped to communicate in silence what was urgently necessary to know. She found her voice. "What was it, Edward?" She spoke in a half-whisper as if they were alone in the room. "What happened?"

"Drink this," he insisted and she realized this was the second time he had said it, and noted that his face was gray and set, his shoulders tensed. "Drink this first."

She moved her arms and the coat fell open and she saw her stained hands and dress. "Oh, Edward—!" She began on a rising note. "Michael—?"

"Miss Mims! Miss Mims, fetch a damp cloth, or a sponge, will you, please?" Like an automaton Miss Mims rose and obeyed him, leaving the room with stiff little steps, her eyes vacantly staring. "And close the door." She shut the door softly.

"Where is he, Edward?"

"In the drawing room still."

In the flowery cave, with his mother. "He's dead, isn't he?"

"Yes, he's dead." Edward pressed the glass to her lips and the hot liquid brought everything surging into focus around her.

"Edward, *what happened?*"

"He was shot."

"Shot? By whom?"

"I don't know. The police have been sent for, and Dr. Burke." And then he set the glass aside and took both her stained hands and folded them together in his and pressed them against his cheek, his eyes shut. "Oh, God, Carlotta." And a pent-up sigh escaped him. "I should never have left you alone."

She shut her eyes also and leaned her cheek comfortingly against his hands, so that their temples touched. But a voice pleaded in the back of her mind, Let it be someone else who did it, but not Dermot, not Dermot. . . .

Miss Mims brought a sponge and they cleaned Carlotta's hands, and then the door was flung open and Dermot, blanched and older of face, his hair incongruously sunny in the atmosphere of death, strode in at the head of a little body of persons, including the policeman with the five-o'clock shadow who had first described Carlotta's mystic feelings. A steady fatalistic bleakness replaced the earlier fury in Dermot's eyes, and they came to rest on Carlotta, and he moved in his careful way to her and placed one hand on her shoulder and asked with a curious, strained formality, "You're all right now?"

"Yes, I'm all right."

He straightened and motioned everyone to be seated. No one questioned his authority, least of all the gentle policeman. Somberly Dermot stood by the mantel, alone, and it came to Carlotta that he was now, at last, the master of Kilraven. Already, perhaps without realizing it, he had assumed the full responsibility of the household. He explained that this was to be but a brief preliminary inquiry, to get some idea of how to proceed. The policeman, his lilting, liquid voice lowered, then asked Carlotta to describe her part "in the sad event," which she did straightforwardly, in a kind of numbness.

"In fact," murmured the policeman at last, his eyes downcast, "it would seem someone did listen at the tower door and went to wait in the drawing room."

Everyone was silent for an instant, and then Miss Mims was saying with a low-pitched ferocity, "Well, it wasn't I!" Her round dark eyes moved, gleaming, over each face. "Quite often I do go up to the upstairs hall at night to—to see that all is well." Her moment of defiance was quickly over; anguish took possession of her. "But tonight I was too exhausted." She caught her lower lip in her teeth, her chin trembled, and with an odd clucking noise she got her breath. "It was the draft wakened me. I sleep with my door open out of habit in case Lady—" She stopped and began again, hoarsely. "I got up to investigate the draft and I had just reached the hall when I saw them, coming down the stairs." Her black eyes fixed themselves on Carlotta. "I saw Mrs. Fleet with Lord Kilraven. I saw her lead him into the drawing room!"

Carlotta stared back incredulously: was Miss Mims accusing her? Softly the policeman prompted, "And then?"

"I listened a moment, and moved closer to the room, and then—and then—" It seemed as if she would stick there, but she cleared her throat and managed to say, "The shot was fired! Oh, no," she said to Carlotta, "I'm not saying you fired it, but you brought him there, you took him out of the tower where he was safe; I warned you—"

"Enough!" said Dermot, so penetratingly that Miss Mims seemed to collapse at once, her elbows pulled in, and she huddled in her chair with her face turned away.

The policeman stirred. "And now, Mr. Fenn, if you would be so good—" And Carlotta felt herself grow suddenly cool, and braced herself.

But it was Edward who spoke. "Perhaps I can expedite matters by telling you that Dermot Fenn and I were together on the south side of the castle when we heard the shot." And Carlotta bowed her head in thankfulness.

There was another silence. All eyes were now downcast. A thousand questions, or one question alone, hung excruciatingly in the air. How much of the truth had Miss Mims told them, or not told them? Until now Carlotta had never felt the emanations of this kind of communal suspicion. And in spite of herself she remembered that it was Miss Mims who had said Michael would be better off dead. Dermot brought his fist down with a crash on the mantel and everyone started, Miss Mims uttering an inverted scream.

At almost the same moment the policeman rose and said, "We must find your wife, Mr. Fenn."

"Yes!" he cried at once, and then folded his arms, his nostrils flaring. "But where, will you tell me that? She's taken herself off, I tell you, her car is missing, she's been gone all the evening!" But some private agony spoke behind his eyes, and now that he was abruptly silent his clenching jaw moved the planes of his cheeks.

"I think she was here," said Miss Mims quietly. She raised her head. "At least," she continued, her regard leveling on Carlotta again, and for some reason the tears began to spill down her face, "I couldn't see who it was who rushed past me in the hall just after the shot—immediately afterward." She seemed unaware of her tears, and something abject in her reluctant honesty reminded Carlotta of the vicar's daughter dutifully cycling in the rain. "I could have sworn—it was—Moira's car."

"Yes," whispered Dermot, "there was a car. I remember." And his voice, like a sigh, held a sound of hopelessness, a confession of foreordained grief.

Carlotta leaned forward.

"What is it?" Edward touched her arm restrainingly.

She was all but spent, she realized; the obliterating numbness threatened to settle on her brain as if forever. The milky light of dawn hovered at the windows and the lamplit room seemed dazzlingly theatrical.

"It's just a feeling," she said, her dry voice in the silent room gathering momentum, and Dermot stared at her with a scowl of misgiving. "Forgive me, Dermot. There may be nothing to it, but I have to say it. It may not be too late. I would look for Moira—at the cliffs of Moher."

She was right, as it turned out, in one sense. They found Moira at the cliffs of Moher. She was wrong in another; it was too late.

12

The car windows were open to a golden day, to a scene of yellow gorse and sparkling brooks and to the sunlit smell of the sea. Edward drove Carlotta in her car again—the faithful little vehicle she would finally surrender at the airport today. The Malloys had taken her off to Rossgharda after the tragedy at Kilraven. She had left her car with Edward, and now at last he had come to fetch her.

A little cavalcade, in fact, set out from Rossgharda this golden day. The Malloys, with Constance Temple and Conor O'Connell, led the way in the Bentley, followed by Carlotta and Edward, and far behind, happy to be outdistanced, Sheilah and Tony brought up the rear in the lime-yellow Fiat. They were all to lunch at Kilraven Castle and then Carlotta and Edward would board the four-o'clock plane for the States.

She was glad Edward had come for her. "I haven't seen you alone since—" she began, and checked herself. "Well, not in days." She still found it hard to name the tragedy.

"Since *Walpurgisnacht*," he offered. "I know; I've missed you, but I thought you needed time for detachment."

"I wonder," she answered quietly. "I haven't brooded about it, or thought about it objectively either, but it goes on behind my thoughts. There've been things I've wanted

176

to say to you, such as expressing sorrow for your own feelings about Michael, and—oh, Edward, thanking you for not punishing me with 'I told you so.' "

His hand covered hers as if pressing silence on her. "It's over. What happened to Michael at the end wasn't nearly as cruel as what happened to him in the beginning. I blame you for nothing; I'm grateful to you for a great deal. And my own feelings about Michael are still, I must confess, professional."

"Yes. I can appreciate that now."

Conversation halted temporarily as they came upon a flock of sheep in the road and threaded their way through the woolly, bleating mass; the black-garbed shepherd gave them a flinty stare; they saluted him apologetically, and were free in the lush and sunlit countryside once more.

"Sheep," mused Carlotta, "have terribly fishy eyes, don't you think?" And then unaccountably she was able to ask, "Edward, how is it at Kilraven now?" She added quickly, "Miss Mims, for instance. Is she going back to England?"

"She is not. She is going to look after Dermot Fenn. This is her role in life. He needs her. Who knows better how to run the castle?"

"Perhaps Dermot will know how to run her."

"Perhaps he'll bully her, which I suspect would be even more to her liking."

And with scarcely a tremor she continued, "And how is Dermot taking it now?"

"He keeps alone a good deal. He's occupied of course with the settlement of the estate. He blames himself for Moira."

"But he mustn't!" She controlled her voice. "Moira always had that potential violence in her—even potential murder."

"Exactly. He blames himself for not suspecting what

she might do, especially after the business of the horse. He knew she held Michael responsible for everything that had gone wrong in their lives. Destroying the horse was a clue to her destroying Michael. Once started she would leave nothing undone. He blames himself for not suspecting she would use the cliffs to destroy herself." He shook his head. "Something more Wagnerian than Greek about this!"

"Something more Irish than Wagnerian," Carlotta said. "Have you read the legends? They're full of frightful slayings. No, I think Moira would have gone over those cliffs sooner or later. I think she wanted to the day of Fran's picnic. I never saw a death wish more clearly." She pondered a moment. "Perhaps he really blames himself for not suspecting that in her tortured way she loved him."

"Loved, Carlotta? I think her torture was the taste of ashes. Yes, perhaps she had loved him once quite passionately. And, to a degree, I think he still loved her."

"Any degree of love is better than no love at all."

He was silent an instant. "Carlotta," he said thoughtfully, "you are forever coming out with the most ridiculous, incontrovertible statements."

She laughed, relieved that he had changed the tone of the conversation. "Bear with me. No doubt you'll have to put up with a few more between now and our arrival in the States."

"I would be happy to put up with them between now and Doomsday."

She turned to him. "Why, Edward," she said quietly, at a loss for words, yet not really surprised.

He removed his pipe and gave her a smiling glance. "Do you feel a degree of love for me?"

"I do, Edward."

He winced. "That was a little too prompt!"

178

"Well, perhaps because I knew it already."

"You're frighteningly calm about it. I don't feel calm about you at all."

"You don't, Edward?"

"And don't tell me it's good for me. I *know* it's good for me, if the complete disruption of my physical and mental being can be considered salutary." Suddenly he dropped his bantering tone. "Carlotta," he said simply, "I adore you. I can't bear you out of my sight or ken. I know I—"

"Edward!" She reached for his hand. "Let's talk about it after we leave. I'm not really myself now. I mean," she said, gazing at the passing emerald fields, the ever-present clouds of the sky, the close and personal sky, "I mean I'm a little taken up with sadness, with saying goodbye."

"To whom, Carlotta?" he asked apprehensively.

"To what. To Ireland."

A moment later her hand tightened on his. "I'm thankful you're going with me. You are very dear to me."

The master of Kilraven sat at the head of the table under the eyes of all the bygone Fenns while his guests kept up a cheerful chatter around him. Dermot was thinner, more dignified in a sense, handsomer, but his gravity was absolute, as if since the tragedy he had taken a vow. It wrung Carlotta's heart, and she hoped the grip of shock and penance would loosen in time. He didn't look at her. On the castle steps, greeting his guests with sober courtesy, his eyes had passed once, swiftly, over her traveling costume, and then he had looked away.

It was a faultless luncheon, with the finest linen, the best wines, a beautifully decorated salmon from Lough Mask. Champagne for toasting had been thought of. Even Lady Kilraven had not presented so kindly a meal. Hannan served with greater intimacy and confidence, as if he had been promoted into a five-star hierarchy of butler-hood, and Miss Mims, subdued, pale, purged, sat in her old place at the foot of the table and kept her eye on everything as her mistress had schooled her to do.

And as if it were more of a housewarming than a fare-well party, the company made a concerted effort to create gaiety. Not a word had been spoken amongst them before-hand on the matter, but they all acted instinctively on the theory that the days of haunting at Kilraven must come to an end. Even Constance Temple, after a long, un-fathomable study of the portrait of Michael, turned to contribute her serene charm. The young couple radiated their own enchantment, and O'Connell played the part of the honored bard with unusual beneficence. Toward the end of the meal, with Dermot's permission, J.J. rose, glass in hand, and began a speech whose appropriateness, he subtly indicated, was due to the commencement of a new regime in the castle.

"Now, we are ostensibly gathered," he continued, look-ing like a bland bull terrier, "to bid Godspeed to Carlotta and Dr. Fabret, but since Ireland must lose one charming pilgrim, descendant of her glorious—"

"Don't get carried away, J.J.," begged Fran.

"I must ask for silence," he protested.

"Hear, hear!" seconded O'Connell, who was already planning an elaborate speech of his own.

"Since, as I was saying, we must lose one charming pilgrim, it is fitting that we welcome as a permanent resident another. I ask you to drink the health of Sheilah Malloy, who will in the near future become Mrs. An-thony Temple."

Even Dermot Fenn broke into a smile at that, there was applause, everyone rose to the toast, the young couple beamed. Tony was prevailed upon to say a few words, which he did so quietly and movingly, with such dignity, his eyes upon Sheilah in her Juliet-like transfiguration, that O'Connell forgot his speech, blew his nose, and merely offered a little Gaelic blessing. The meal concluded at last in laughter.

As they left the room Fran fell into step beside Dermot Fenn. "We're house-hunting, you know. J.J. and I will be needing a berth over here."

Dermot's blue eyes moved sideways to her with an amused glimmer. "Are you now?"

"Castle-hunting," said J.J., with a sigh, behind them, "is what she really means."

"And of course we'd need you to take care of it for us," Fran plunged blithely on. "Well, after all, what's the use of beating about the bush? There was talk once of selling Kilraven to Americans, and we'd like first refusal."

"She's never recovered from being Lady Malloy," said J.J.

"I'll not commit myself now," Dermot told her.

"Of course not," replied Fran, with a grin. "But having us here once in a while would be better than turning it into a hotel, wouldn't it?"

"By far," agreed Dermot soberly.

"That's enough, Mrs. Malloy," commanded J.J. "Be off with you. I'll do the talking." And he and Dermot strolled away toward the library. There was still time to kill before leaving for Shannon, and the guests were idly scattering in little groups.

Carlotta had moved to the stairs in search of Mary, her former maid, and Fran caught up with her. "Maybe I shouldn't have blurted it out like that, I'll probably catch hell from J.J., but Dermot seemed in a better mood just then, and well, you know me and my big mouth."

"It's a delightful idea," Carlotta told her, grateful for her wholesome company, eclipsing memories. They

181

were mounting the great staircase. "Fran, your very own castle!"

"And you would visit us!" said Fran, linking arms. "Of course it would need some improvement, heat-wise and private-bathroom-wise, but basically we wouldn't want to change it. Keep your fingers crossed."

They found Mary of the flaming cheeks and Carlotta bade her goodbye. Mary wept sentimentally into her apron for a second or two and then laughed, pocketing a pound note. Was it true that Lady Malloy was after taking over the castle? Fran hooted. One thing hadn't changed at Kilraven; news traveled as fast as ever. Ah God, said Mary, perhaps there was to be some joy in the place at last! They all embraced.

Dermot was waiting in the hall downstairs. "Between the two of you Malloys," he told Fran dryly, "ye'll have the place from me yet. At least ye've got your first refusal." And she hurried off to the library in search of J.J. It was good to hear Dermot's old half-insolent dialect. But with his new gravity he said to Carlotta, "The others are strolling out of doors. Shall we go and find them?"

He led her wordlessly to the walled garden. He knew, of course, that the others had taken another direction. He closed the wooden door and leaned against it. The enclosure was heavy with rose-scent and the concentrated hum of bees. His blue eyes rested fully on Carlotta at last. He said, simply, "Stay with me."

She had half-turned away, and now she faced him quickly, bringing her hands together in distress. "Dermot, I can't do that."

"Stay with me, Carleen. Don't leave."

"But I have to. My home is in the States, I must go back!"

"Stay with me."

"Anyway, it's too soon after—"

182

"Yes, it's too soon after, but you can stop at Rossgharda with Constance, and later, after the young ones marry, you and I can have a quiet wedding of our own."

"Oh, Dermot, don't," she pleaded. "I mustn't think of it now, Ireland isn't quite real to me now——"

"Isn't quite real to you?" He took a step forward and caught her hard in his arms. "I'd make it real to you soon enough."

She tried to draw away from him. "At least let me go back and think about it. Somehow I must get my feet on the ground again!"

"If you go now you'll never come back. Once you get your feet on the ground I will seem unreal to you, too. Stay with me! I have love to give you, Carlotta, I have much love to give you. Is it love for me that you lack?"

Her eyes filled suddenly. "It isn't love for you that I lack. It's just that——" His arms tightened, his lips stopped the words. She summoned all her strength, all remaining common sense. "But I must go back! I would have to go back in any case!"

"You'll end up marrying Edward Fabret, a decent fellow altogether, and neither of us will ever know the depths and breadth of love. No, it's a region I've never explored, and you have never explored it with me. The whole heart's love, Carleen——"

"I have to go back, I have to go back." She could never explain it to him, in this state she could hardly explain it to herself. But just as he had instinctively taken his place at the head of Kilraven, she had to respect the responsibilities of her own life. How could she make a decision involving so much reality while she was still under the spell of this island? "I have to!"

There was a flurry of kissing at the barrier to the plane. " 'Cast a cold eye,' " advised O'Connell, a little fuzzily, his noble, lumpy face all sageness, and he winked, " 'on life, on death.' "

"Take care of her," J.J. warned Edward with mock severity, "or you'll have me to answer to."

"If you think you're saying goodbye to us you're crazy!" said Fran, throwing her arms around Carlotta in a great hug.

"There'll always be a welcome at Rossgharda," Constance crooned. "Put the bad memories out of your mind and remember only the glad ones."

"Of course you'll be at our wedding," said Tony handsomely, as if it were a joy she couldn't possibly deny herself.

"Love-love," murmured Sheilah, putting up her soft cheek.

Dermot took her hand. Again a little smile lightened the burden of his face. "Come back," he told her in a low voice. "I'll be waiting."

Just before they boarded the plane Carlotta turned once more and waved, her eyes blurred.

"You don't have to say goodbye," Edward told her quietly, waving also. "You can come back, you know."

"Yes, I can."

"Will you?" he asked. "Will you come back?" He hesitated. "Or isn't there any sense in asking you now?"

She smiled in spite of her heavy heart. He had acknowledged the wait-and-see policy that Harry had found so exasperating. Edward knew she was so constituted that she could not find the answer unless she waited for it, and unless she waited for it it would not be the right one. "No," she told him gratefully. "There isn't."

She closed her eyes for an instant and took a deep breath through her nostrils: yes, there it was, the scent of peat smoke she had recognized in her bones when she arrived. And suddenly she saw that person as a stranger, arriving that faraway day—small, as if seen through the wrong end of a telescope; naïve, loveless, locked in a tiny, timorous world.

How could she say goodbye to a land, a people, who had given her herself?

"Shall we go then, Carlotta?"

"Yes." She took his arm and they turned and went aboard.